Peter Grant

Emblems of Jesus

Or, illustrations of Emmanuel's Character and Work

SALZWASSER
VERLAG

Peter Grant

Emblems of Jesus

Or, illustrations of Emmanuel's Character and Work

Reprint of the original, first published in 1863.

1st Edition 2022 | ISBN: 978-3-37500-659-4

Verlag (Publisher): Salzwasser Verlag GmbH, Zeilweg 44, 60439 Frankfurt, Deutschland
Vertretungsberechtigt (Authorized to represent): E. Roepke, Zeilweg 44, 60439 Frankfurt, Deutschland
Druck (Print): Books on Demand GmbH, In de Tarpen 42, 22848 Norderstedt, Deutschland

EMBLEMS OF JESUS.

EMBLEMS OF JESUS;

OR,

ILLUSTRATIONS OF EMMANUEL'S CHARACTER AND WORK.

"There's not a strain to memory dear,
Nor flower in classic grove,
There's not a sweet note warbled here,
But minds us of Thy love.
O Lord, our Lord, and spoiler of our foes,
There is no light but Thine; with Thee all beauty glows."

KEBLE.

1863.

PREFACE.

THE object of the present volume is to illustrate a few of the many striking and beautiful Emblems by which the Scriptures shadow forth the matchless excellences of our Emmanuel, and the blessedness of possessing a personal interest in His great salvation.

Although the subject of sacred metaphors in general has doubtless often been handled by others, yet the Author is not aware of any existing work that is specially devoted to the elucidation of emblems descriptive of the character and work of

Jesus Christ. He has, therefore, gathered together and illustrated a few of this latter class; and if, by the blessing of God, his humble labours shall be instrumental in endearing the Saviour to the souls of his readers, it will be to him more than recompense.

P. G.

November 1863.

CONTENTS.

PAGE

THE HIDING-PLACE FROM THE STORM, . . 9

THE MORNING STAR, ... 23

THE PLANT OF RENOWN, ... 39

THE SUN OF RIGHTEOUSNESS, ... 55

THE TRUE MANNA, ... 69

THE SMITTEN ROCK, ... 85

THE BRAZEN SERPENT, ... 109

THE PASCHAL LAMB, ... 123

THE GOEL; OR, KINSMAN REDEEMER, . . 139

THE CITY OF REFUGE, ... 155

THE GOOD SHEPHERD, ... 175

THE PHYSICIAN, ... 193

CONCLUSION, ... 209

The Hiding-place from the Storm.

2 SAM. xxii. 2, 3.

"And he said, The Lord is my rock, and my fortress, and my deliverer; the God of my rock; in him will I trust: he is my shield, and the horn of my salvation, my high tower, and my refuge, my Saviour; thou savest me from violence."

Ps. lvii. 1.

"Be merciful unto me, O God, be merciful unto me; for my soul trusteth in thee: yea, in the shadow of thy wings will I make my refuge, until these calamities be overpast."

Ps. xxxii. 7.

"Thou art my hiding-place; thou shalt preserve me from trouble; thou shalt compass me about with songs of deliverance."

ISA. xxv. 4.

"For thou hast been a strength to the poor, a strength to the needy in his distress, a refuge from the storm, a shadow from the heat, when the blast of the terrible ones is as a storm against the wall."

ISA. xxxii. 2.

"And a man shall be as an hiding-place from the wind, and a covert from the tempest; as rivers of water in a dry place; as the shadow of a great rock in a weary land."

GAL. iii. 13.

"Christ hath redeemed us from the curse of the law, being made a curse for us: for it is written, Cursed is every one that hangeth on a tree."

HEB. ix. 28.

"So Christ was once offered to bear the sins of many."

"Jesus, lover of my soul,
Let me to Thy mercy fly,
While the raging billows roll,
While the tempest still is high;
Hide me, O my Saviour, hide,
Till the storm of life is past;
Safe into the haven guide;
Oh, receive my soul at last!

"Other refuge have I none,
Hangs my helpless soul on Thee;
Leave, ah! leave me not alone,
Still support and comfort me;
All my trust on Thee is stay'd,
All my help from Thee I bring;
Cover my defenceless head
With the shadow of Thy wing.

"Thou, O Lord, art all I want;
All in all in Thee I find;
Raise the fallen, cheer the faint,
Heal the sick, and lead the blind.
Just and holy is Thy name,
I am all unrighteousness;
Vile and full of sin I am,
Thou art full of truth and grace.

"Plenteous grace with Thee is found,
Grace to pardon all my sin;
Let the healing streams abound,
Make and keep me pure within.
Thou of life the fountain art;
Freely let me take of Thee;
Spring Thou up within my heart,
Rise to all eternity!"

WESLEY.

THE HIDING-PLACE FROM THE STORM.

MANY Scripture emblems are borrowed from the dreary region of the Arabian desert, to which the sacred writers so frequently refer as the scene of Israel's wanderings. Among these, that placed at the head of this chapter is by no means the least appropriate or instructive. It is not possible, perhaps, for us to appreciate its full force, living, as we do, under a temperate climate, and in a country almost universally cultivated. But this metaphor must have been felt with great power by the inhabitants of Judea who lived in the vicinity of the desert, and who had probably often witnessed the ravages of those overwhelming winds and tempests which ever and anon swept across it. Hence the language of Isaiah, when he spake of "a man who should be as an hiding-place from the wind, and a covert from the tempest," must have conveyed to them the liveliest idea of the protection that was to be derived from the promised Messiah, even "the man Christ Jesus." The prophet seems to have had in view the condition of a traveller passing through the desert when swept by a fierce wind, which threatens to overwhelm him by its fury, but, in his extremity, discovering a hiding-place and covert within his reach, to which, with eager gladness, he flees, and where he dwells in safety till the storm is overpast. Such is the emblem by which the prophet represents the shelter and security which believers find in Christ, amid the fierce and frequent storms, to which they are exposed when passing through the "waste howling wilderness" of this world, and which threaten to overwhelm them with their sweeping and resistless tide.

This emblem suggests that "the man Christ Jesus" is the believer's security amidst *the storms of earthly trouble and affliction.* Ere sin entered our world, the firmament of man's existence was cloudless and serene; but, by reason of His apostasy, the earth has been converted into a wilderness, full of storms and tempests ; and no sooner is one source of agitation and disquietude dried up, than another is forthwith let loose upon us. From one quarter issue forth the chilling winds of adversity, which frustrate all our designs, and blast all our expectations ; from another descend the storms of affliction, which fill our hearts with the most poignant grief, and beneath whose pressure we are weighed to the dust. From all points are incessantly blowing the pestilential winds of Satan's temptations, by which at first Eden itself was laid waste, and which are still directed against us with the utmost subtlety and violence, in order that the house of our hope may be shaken and fall, and that of our faith we may be driven to make shipwreck. And did we not know, amidst all these storms with which we are assailed, where to find shelter and security, our case would be infinitely worse than that of the desert-pilgrim, who pursues his solitary way all unprotected, and exposed to the pitiless pelting of the storm, without any rock or covert within his view over all the illimitable waste. But, blessed be God, "the man Christ Jesus" is a stronghold and hiding-place, in which we may safely repose, until the blasts and convulsions of calamity be overpast. There we are secure alike from the arrow that flieth in darkness, and from the destruction that rageth at noonday. That Refuge has defied all blasts, and stood in the face of all storms. Generation after generation has sat under its shadow; and the fathers to the children have told, as the fathers to the children continue to tell, that, from the assaults and fury of the world, "from the pride of man, and from the strife of tongues," from the desolating tempests which the Wicked One is permitted to raise in the believer's soul, it is an almighty and seasonable defence. Such has been the happy experience of thousands, who have gone before us in this vale of tears. Amidst the wildest and most appalling storms of earthly trouble, they were "kept in perfect peace, because their minds were stayed on Him." They knew that it was His Spirit that guided the whirlwind and rode upon the storm, and that His hand of mercy was in all the afflictions which befell them, making them instrumental in promoting their truest and most permanent good. To Him, therefore, did they flee, as unto a sanctuary;

and, believing His truths, and relying on His infinite power to protect, and His infinite beneficence to bless them, they possessed their souls in patience and in peace.

The emblem under consideration suggests, also, that "the man Christ Jesus" is the believer's security against *the storm of Jehovah's wrath.* All the temporal storms to which we have adverted are but as drops before the shower when compared with the terrible storm of wrath which is in store for the ungodly and unbelieving. Of that future storm we can form but a very faint and inadequate conception. "Who knoweth the power of thine anger? According to thy fear, so is thy wrath." The Word of God shadows it forth by images the most terrific. "On the wicked," it is declared, God "shall rain snares, fire and brimstone, and an horrible tempest; this shall be the portion of their cup." "A fire is kindled in mine anger, and it shall burn unto the lowest hell." Need we marvel, then, that when an individual seriously considers how fearful a thing it is to fall into the hands of the living God, he should cry out, as in an agony of alarm, "What must I do to be saved?" For "who can dwell with the devouring fire? Who can dwell with the everlasting burnings?" Aroused to a sense of his guilt and danger, he looks around for a place of refuge from the whirlwind of that Divine wrath which "is revealed from heaven against all unrighteousness and ungodliness of men." But, alas! every earthly refuge is unavailing, and would inevitably be swept away by the overflowing deluge. He is ready to rush into the arms of despair; when, behold, God, whose wrath and condemnation he had incurred, comes down to him, and reveals a system of mercy and salvation, which, while it abates nothing of wrath to the finally impenitent, secures pardon and peace to those who "repent, and believe His gospel." A Refuge is provided, whose foundation is the Rock of Ages, and beneath whose shadow no wind or tempest can assail us. Jesus, the Son of the Highest, is our hiding-place from the wind, and our covert from the tempest of Divine indignation.

The Word of God clearly reveals to us, both the manner in which He has effected our deliverance and the mode in which we become interested in His mediatorial work. "God hath reconciled us to himself by Jesus Christ, and hath given to us the ministry of reconciliation, to wit, that God was in Christ, reconciling the world unto himself, not imputing their trespasses unto them." "He was wounded for our transgressions, bruised for our iniquities; the chastisement of our peace was upon him, that by his stripes we might be healed." It thus appears, that the means by which sinners are delivered from the wrath to come, was by Jesus bearing that wrath Himself in our room and stead. He "suffered, the just for the unjust, that He might bring us to God."

Not less plainly revealed is the manner in which we become interested in His great deliverance. It is by believing on His name. "Behold, I lay in Zion a foundation, he that believeth shall not make haste." "Believing, we shall have life through His name." "He that believeth in Him is not condemned, but hath everlasting life." If we do but possess this faith, we need fear no evil. "There is, therefore, now no condemnation to them that are in Christ Jesus." "Being justified by faith, they have peace with God, through our Lord

Jesus Christ." The very name of Jesus is unto them as a strong tower; they run into it, and are safe. The sanctuary of His mediation is a defence, "stronger than the munition of rocks;" "they shall never perish, neither shall any pluck them out of His hand." They "dwell in a peaceable habitation, and in sure dwellings, and in quiet resting-places." "Because they have made the Lord who is their refuge, even the Most High their habitation, there shall no evil befall them, neither shall any plague come nigh their dwelling." "The Lord shall preserve them from all evil."

How thankful ought we to be to Almighty God, for His infinite goodness and mercy in raising up for us a Refuge and Hiding-place that thus effectually screens and protects us from every storm by which we can be overtaken or threatened. Let us, then, "give thanks unto the Lord, for he is good; for his mercy endureth for ever."

Let it be remembered, however, that shelter and security are to be found only in Christ. How unspeakable, then, must be the misery and the danger of those who are none of His! Not only are they tossed upon a sea of earthly trouble, but they stand unsheltered from the terrific storm gathering against them—even the wrath to come—wrath still coming, but never all come; a storm that shall beat upon them throughout the ages of eternity.

Reader, what will become of you, should death overtake you in this defenceless state —while out of Christ, the only effectual hiding-place? Whither will you flee for help or shelter? Will you call on the rocks and mountains to fall on you, and hide you from the face of Him who sitteth on the throne, and from the wrath of the Lamb? The mountains shall fly away, and the hills melt like wax, before the God of the whole earth. If Christ be not your hiding-place, destruction must inevitably overtake you. Flee, then, to Him. "Be of good comfort;" O sinner, "rise, He calleth thee." Into this refuge, all, without exception, are invited to enter; here even the chief of sinners may obtain a welcome. Think not of betaking yourself to any other shelter, in the vain hope that the storm of Divine indignation will leave it undisturbed. This were but to increase your danger; for, in place of protection, it would prove a snare. No refuge but that sought for in the arms of Christ will be found strong enough against the storm and tempest. Give all diligence, then, to be found in Him, that so "in the time of trouble He may hide you in His pavilion; that in the secret of His tabernacle He may hide you, and set you upon a rock."

Blessed, blessed beyond compare, are all those who have taken sanctuary in Him! Nothing from without can harm or affright them any more. The eternal God is their refuge; underneath and around them are the Saviour's everlasting arms. Their peace can never be removed. External circumstances —the loss of fortune, of fame, of health—do not impair it; they rather confirm its exercise, and render its value more sensibly evident, like "the storm howling o'er the well-stayed battlements," which only enhances the sense of comfort to those who are lodged within. The rains may descend, the floods beat, and the winds blow, but it abides unshaken, for it is founded upon the "Rock of Ages."

"Betake thee to thy Christ, then, and repose
Thyself, in all extremities, on those
His everlasting arms,

Wherewith He girds the heavens, and upholds
The pillars of the earth, and safely folds
His faithful flock from harms,
Cleave close to Him by faith, and let the bands
Of love tie thee in thy Redeemer's hands."

QUARLES.

"Jesus, to Thee, my sure defence,
My help for ever nigh,
From the rough blast and rushing storm
For shelter I apply.

"Thou art my only hiding-place,
Thou my secure abode,
When vengeance like a whirlwind flies,
And rages all abroad.

"As rocks to guard from burning skies
Their ample shades extend,
Do Thou from flames of wrath divine
My guilty soul defend."

"God in Christ, Jehovah-Jesus,
God with us in human form,
This shall be my ark of refuge,
This my rock in every storm;
Here I shelter from the wrath-cloud,
Here repose like trustful child,
For 'tis here I view my Maker
As my Father reconciled."

RUTH WILLS.

"Awake, sweet harp of Judah, wake,
Retune thy strings for Jesus' sake;
We sing the Saviour of our race,
The Lamb, our shield and hiding-place.

"'Tis He, the Lamb, to whom we fly,
While the dread tempest passes by;
God sees His well-beloved's face,
And spares us in our hiding-place.

"Yet courage, days and years will glide;
And guilt and frailty laid aside,
We shall be borne o'er Jordan's flood,
Our robes made white in Jesus' blood.

"Then, pure, immortal, sinless, freed,
We through the Lamb shall be decreed,
Shall meet our Father face to face,
And need no more a hiding-place."

H. K. White.

The Morning Star.

NUM. xxiv. 17.

"I shall see him, but not now; I shall behold him, but not nigh: there shall come a star out of Jacob, and a sceptre shall rise out of Israel."

ISA. lx. 1–3.

"Arise, shine; for thy light is come, and the glory of the Lord is risen upon thee. For, behold, the darkness shall cover the earth, and gross darkness the people: but the Lord shall arise upon thee, and his glory shall be seen upon thee. And the Gentiles shall come to thy light, and kings to the brightness of thy rising."

ISA. lx. 19.

"The sun shall be no more thy light by day; neither for brightness shall the moon give light unto thee: but the Lord shall be unto thee an everlasting light, and thy God thy glory."

LUKE i. 78, 79.

"Through the tender mercy of our God, whereby the day-spring from on high hath visited us, to give light to them that sit in darkness, and in the shadow of death, to guide our feet into the way of peace.'

2 PET. i. 19.

"We have also a more sure word of prophecy; whereunto ye do well that ye take heed, as unto a light that shineth in a dark place, until the day dawn, and the day-star arise in your hearts."

REV. xxii. 16.

"I am the root and the offspring of David, and the bright and morning star."

"When, marshall'd on the nightly plain,
The glittering host bestud the sky,
One star alone, of all the train,
Can fix the sinner's wandering eye.

"Hark! hark! to God the chorus breaks,
From every host, from every gem;
But one alone the Saviour speaks,
It is the Star of Bethlehem.

"Once on the raging seas I rode;
The storm was loud—the night was dark—
The ocean yawn'd—and rudely blow'd
The wind that toss'd my foundering bark.

"Deep horror then my vitals froze;
Death-struck, I ceased the tide to stem;
When suddenly a star arose,—
It was the Star of Bethlehem.

"It was my guide, my light, my all,
It bade my dark forebodings cease;
And through the storm, and dangers' thrall,
It led me to the port of peace.

"Now safely moor'd, my perils o'er,
I'll sing, first in night's diadem,
For ever and for evermore,
The Star, the Star of Bethlehem!"

H. K. White.

THE MORNING STAR

OF all the planets which bestud the firmament, the morning star is, and ever has been, the most admired, on account of her singular brightness and beauty. Though her radiance is not to be compared with that which the sun, or even the moon, casts abroad, yet, in the gorgeous jewellery of the heavens, does she form one of the loveliest gems, while, at particular periods, she shines with a lustre that renders her distinctly visible to the naked eye, several hours after the ruler of the day has arisen upon the earth. But that which chiefly deserves our present attention is, that she is designed not only to beautify the vault of heaven, and to emit light, as do the other "watchers of the sky," but to be, as it were, the sun's harbinger, declaring his speedy approach. When night has encircled the world with its sable mantle, she arises in the heavens, sheds her first light, and ushers in the day. In this respect, she constitutes a strikingly appropriate emblem of our Lord. Accordingly, at the close of His revelation to the Church, we find Him declaring, "I am the bright and morning star." Nor is it difficult to discover the grounds on which He deserves this peculiarly beautiful appellation.

Jesus is the bright and morning star, because, *by His first rising upon the earth, He introduced to its benighted inhabitants the gospel day.* Prior to His appearing on the eastern horizon, the world was enveloped in the gloom of midnight. Mankind had become "vain in their imaginations, and their foolish heart was darkened." Darkness covered the earth, and gross darkness the nations; and though a beam from the Divine glory had shone on the heights of Zion, and gilded for a season the mountains of Israel, yet the clouds and shadows of the ancient dispensation veiled it from the view of the faithful, while upon the great bulk of the Jewish people there had settled down a deep and impenetrable gloom of vice and superstition.

But this state of things was not to continue

for ever. The Morning Star at length arose, and the shadows of night began gradually to disperse before His ascending glory. Then "the people that sat in darkness saw great light; and upon them that dwelt in the land of the shadow of death the light shined." Christ's appearing was the fulfilment of God's gracious promise unto the fathers, and the blessed manifestation of His rich favour and goodness to the children of men. Accordingly, the devout Simeon, who waited for "the consolation of Israel," no sooner beheld the child Jesus brought into the temple to be presented after the law, than he exclaimed, "Lord, now lettest thou thy servant depart in peace, according to thy word; for mine eyes have seen thy salvation, which thou hast prepared before the face of all people, to be a light to lighten the Gentiles, and the glory of thy people Israel." At the appearing of this Star, which, according to the ancient oracle, came out of Jacob, the believing expectations of the pious Israelites were fully realised, and the mystery, which had been hid for ages, was made manifest. Before the beams of His glorious gospel, the mists of ignorance and idolatry were dispelled, and the clouds and shadows of the law entirely and for ever disappeared. Enlightened by His rays, the apostles went forth, proclaiming peace through the blood of the cross, exhorting all men everywhere to repent, and offering eternal life to as many as believed on the name of the Lord Jesus. And how great were the multitudes who, through their instrumentality, were brought out of darkness unto light, and from the power of Satan to God! As the light-bearers of Heaven, they not only held forth the Word of life to the inhabitants of Judea, but went forth into all parts of the habitable world. And how many myriads have since been privileged to rejoice in the glorious light of that Dayspring from on high, which, through the tender mercy of our God, hath visited us!

But Jesus further resembles the morning star, as, *by His arising upon our hearts, He ushers in the day of salvation.* Although the true light now shineth in the world, yet the natural mind is in a state of complete darkness and blindness as to the things of God. "The light shineth in darkness, and the darkness comprehendeth it not." Though ready to imbibe the knowledge of things visible and vain, mankind, in their unregenerate state, are averse to listen to, or to know, things invisible and divine. Nor can the light of unassisted reason ever enable them to discover those truths which it is most needful for them to know and believe; and until "He who commanded the light to shine out of darkness, hath shined in their hearts, to give the light of the knowledge of the glory of God in the face of Jesus Christ," their way is as darkness; they see not whither they are going, and must inevitably stumble and fall. Till then, even the light that is in them is darkness.

But when the bright and morning star arises upon the benighted soul, the mists of ignorance, error, and unbelief, are rolled away, and spiritual and eternal objects are beheld in all their transcendent magnitude and importance. By this blessed light are discovered the evil of sin, and the manner of becoming interested in the great salvation,—the nature of faith in Christ, and repentance towards God,—the duties of holy living, and the means of dying in peace and hope,—the glories and felicities of heaven, and the horrors and agonies of hell. Nor does Jesus merely reveal these things; He also opens men's eyes to behold them. While removing their natural ignorance, He at the same time, by the enlightening and purifying influences of His Holy Spirit, enables them clearly to understand, firmly to believe, and ardently to love, His glorious gospel. Thus, in His light do they see light; and encompassed with His cheering beams, they rejoice with exceeding joy.

Oh, how blessed a thing it is to be thus turned from darkness into marvellous light; and with what intense emotions of gratitude should we look back to the period when the day dawned, and the day-star arose in our hearts! You may speak of the gratitude of the tempest-tossed mariner, when, after buffeting the raging of the billows, during the darkness and horrors of a winter's night, his eyes are first blessed with the sight of the morning star, shining forth like a beauteous beacon in the sky,—you may talk of the gratitude of the slave, when the last link of his fetters is thrown away, and he stands forth in the dignity and with the glory of freedom,—you may tell of the gratitude of the condemned criminal, when, at the very scaffold, he hears the announcement of a free and unexpected pardon ;—but all the comparisons which you can heap together, and all the similitudes that you can bring from the ample storehouses of experience, are but faint and feeble illustrations of the gratitude and joy which should spring up in the hearts of those who, from the darkness and desolation of the night of ignorance and sin, have been brought into the marvellous light of the gospel, and made to rejoice in its saving beams.

Again, Jesus resembles the morning star, as *He is the precursor of a day of millennial brightness.* It is doubtless matter of deepest thankfulness to God, that the light of the glorious gospel has already been diffused over so large a portion of our once benighted world ; but we have, at the same time, reason to mourn, that even now, its illumination is very far from being universal. Full many a dark place still exists, which has never yet been visited by the Dayspring from on high, while others, which were once enlightened, are left in midnight darkness. Not seldom, too, even in Christian lands, have we reason to lament with the prophet, "Woe unto us, for the day goeth away; for the shadows of the evening are stretched out." By superstition in some places, by most pernicious errors in others, and by vice in all, the Morning Star is shorn of its brightest rays.

But were the signs of the times even more dark and ominous than they are, we are privileged to exult in the anticipation of another and more glorious day—a day of which the prophets have so sweetly sung, when every region on which the natural sun shines shall be illuminated by the beams of evangelical truth; when the heathen shall fear the name of the Lord, and all the kings of the earth His glory; when the fulness of the Gentiles shall be come in, and all Israel shall be saved; when the glory of the Lord shall be revealed, and all flesh shall see it together; for the mouth of the Lord hath spoken it. Then shall the bright and morning Star again arise upon the benighted nations, and shed His unclouded radiance over every land. His appearing shall be "as the light of the morning, when the sun riseth, even a morning without clouds;" the welcome harbinger of a serene, and bright, and joyous day.

What Christian heart does not bound with holy joy, at the contemplation of such a prospect? In a day like this, when the eye is pained by scenes of misery and desolation, and the heart agonised by the errors, the crimes, and the enormities, with which the earth's surface is darkened, is it not delightful to think, that the bright and morning Star shall yet usher in a day, when our world, cursed by sin, and so long the theatre of human misery, will become like unto the paradise of God, the abode of happiness and joy? Oh! let us unite in fervent prayer, and zealous endeavours, for the arrival of this blessed and glorious era. Be it ours to press forward to "the help of the Lord, to the help of the Lord against the mighty." The cause is great, but the promise is sure. "The wilderness and the solitary place shall be glad for them, and the desert shall rejoice and blossom as the rose. It shall blossom abundantly and rejoice even with joy and singing; the glory of Lebanon shall be given unto it, the excellency of Carmel and Sharon; they shall see the glory of the Lord, and the excellency of our God." The Lord hath said it, and shall He not do it? Is He not doing it before our eyes? Is He not, even now, magnifying His name in the sight of the heathen? "For Zion's sake," then, "let us not hold our peace, and for Jerusalem's sake let us not rest, until the righteousness thereof go forth as brightness, and the salvation thereof as a lamp that burneth."

But Jesus still further resembles the morning star, as *He is the harbinger of eternal day.* Even as the morning star gives promise of the dawn of day, and, rising in brightness, at length blends her lustre with the glories of the heavens, so the light, which the day-spring from on high will shed over every part of the earth's surface at the millennium, is as but the faint glimmering of the twilight, in comparison of the full blaze of glory, into which it will at length melt away, when Jesus shall shine forth, in the centre of the heavenly world, "as the sun in his strength." Then shall a day of perfect knowledge, purity, and happiness commence, upon which the shades of evening shall never close. "And I saw the holy city, new Jerusalem, coming down from God out of heaven, prepared as a bride adorned for her husband; and the city had no need of the light of the sun, neither of the moon to shine in it; for the glory of God did lighten it, and the Lamb is the light thereof. And the nations of them which are saved shall walk in the light of it; and the kings of the earth do bring their glory and honour into it; and the gates of it shall not be shut at all by day: for there shall be no night there." Whatever may here occasion darkness, shall be for ever removed from that glorious world of joy. Neither ignorance, nor unbelief, nor sin can ever find an entrance there. There, "light is sown for the righteous, and gladness for the upright in heart." Nor shall the Lord ever again withdraw from His children the experience of His presence and love. "Their sun shall no more go down, neither shall their moon withdraw itself; for the Lord shall be their everlasting light, and the days of their mourning shall be ended."

If this bright and morning Star has not yet arisen upon our hearts, to guide our feet into the way of peace, let us "give glory to God, ere our feet stumble on the dark mountains" of eternal ruin, "lest, while we look for light, he turn it into the shadow of death, and make it gross darkness." Let us follow the light of truth, now shining around us, which will guide our souls to Jesus, for pardon and peace. "I am the light of the world," He says; "He that followeth me, shall not walk in darkness, but shall have the light of life."

If, on the other hand, we have been enlightened by this blessed luminary, it behoves us to walk, as "children of light." Whilst, therefore, we have no fellowship with the unfruitful works of darkness, be it ours to shine as lights in the world, and shew forth to men around us the glories of Him who hath enlightened us. In our several spheres, and according to the opportunities given us, and the talents bestowed upon us, let us help forward the God-like work of enlightening this dark world—of drawing all men to Christ, the true Light—in the unity of the Spirit, and in the bond of peace, and in righteousness of life.

"Ye worlds of light, that roll so near
The Saviour's throne of shining bliss,
Oh, tell how mean your glories are,
How faint, and few, compared with His.

"We sing the bright and morning Star,
(Jesus, the spring of light and love:)
See how its rays diffused from far,
Conduct us to the realms above.

"Its cheering beams, spread wide abroad,
Point out the troubled Christian's way;
Still, as he goes, he finds the road
Enlighten'd with a constant day.

"Thus when the Eastern magi brought
Their royal gifts, a star appears,
Directs them to the Babe they sought,
And guides their steps, and calms their fears.

"When shall we reach the heavenly place,
Where this bright Star will brightest shine;
Leave far behind these scenes of night,
And view a lustre so divine?" BEDDOME.

"Sceptre and Star divine,
Who in Thine inmost shrine
Hast made us worshippers, oh, claim Thine own;
More than Thy seers we know,
Oh, teach our love to grow
Up to Thy heavenly light, and reap what Thou hast sown."
KEBLE.

"Thou art the life, O Lord!
Sole light of life Thou art!
Let not Thy glorious rays be pour'd
In vain on my dark heart.

"Star of the East, arise!
Drive all my clouds away,
Guide me till earth's dim twilight dies
Into the perfect day!"

LAURENTI, 1700.

"The light of reason cannot give
Life to my soul;
Jesus alone can make me truly live,
One glance of His can make my spirit whole.
Arise and shine,
O Jesus, on this longing heart of mine.

"Single and clear, not weak or blind,
The eye must be,
To which Thy glory shall an entrance find;
For if Thy chosen ones would gaze on Thee,
No earthly screen
Between their souls and Thee must intervene.

"Jesus, do thou mine eyes unseal,
And let them grow
Quick to discern whate'er Thou dost reveal,
So shall I be deliver'd from that woe,
Blindly to stray
Through hopeless night, while all around is day."

RICHTER, 1704

The Plant of Renown.

ISA. xi. 1.

"And there shall come forth a rod out of the stem of Jesse and a Branch shall grow out of his roots."

CANT. ii. 1, 2, 3.

"I am the rose of Sharon, and the lily of the valleys. As the lily among thorns, so is my love among the daughters. As the apple tree among the trees of the wood, so is my beloved among the sons. I sat down under his shadow with great delight, and his fruit was sweet to my taste."

JER. xxiii. 5.

"Behold, the days come, saith the Lord, that I will raise unto David a righteous Branch, and a King shall reign and prosper."

EZEK. xvi. 14.

"And thy renown went forth among the heathen for thy beauty: for it was perfect through my comeliness, which I had put upon thee, saith the Lord God."

EZEK. xxxiv. 29.

"And I will raise up for them a Plant of renown, and they shall no more be consumed with hunger in the land, neither bear the shame of the heathen any more."

EZEK. xlvii. 12.

"And by the river, upon the bank thereof, on this side and on that side, shall grow all trees for meat, whose leaf shall not fade, neither shall the fruit thereof be consumed: it shall bring forth new fruit according to his months, because their waters they issued out of the sanctuary; and the fruit thereof shall be for meat, and the leaf thereof for medicine."

"Sweeter is Jesus' love to me
  Than Sharon's fragrant rose,
He lovelier than the lily is
  That in the valley grows.

"Fair as amid the forest wide
  The citron tree is seen,
So, fairer than the sons of men
  He in my sight has been.

"I sat in His refreshing shade,
  My weary soul to rest;
His fruit revived my soul again,
  And sweet was to my taste.

"He brought me to His banquet house,
  A costly feast He made;
And lo! the banner of His love
  He over me did spread.

"Cheer me with wine, with odours sweet,
  My fainting soul restore;
For I am vanquish'd by His love,
  The love to me He bore."

M'CONKCHY.

THE PLANT OF RENOWN.

THIS emblem, under the veil of which our blessed Redeemer is introduced by the prophet Ezekiel, is widely different from that which Isaiah applies to Him, when he speaks of the promised Messiah "growing up as a tender plant, and as a root out of a dry ground." Yet, a very little consideration is sufficient to satisfy us, that, between these two views of Christ, there is really nothing in the slightest degree incongruous, much less contradictory. They refer to different parts of His wondrous history. In the one, Isaiah describes the obscurity of His origin and His life of unparalleled humiliation, while, in the other, the allusion is to His subsequent exaltation, when He, who, as a rejected root, had been bruised and trampled under the feet of men, should become greatly renowned on earth, by the spread of His glorious gospel throughout all nations.

In our present contemplation of this celestial Plant, we shall restrict ourselves to an illustration of a few of those excellences, on which its renown is founded.

This Plant, then, we begin by remarking, is justly renowned on account of its surpassing *beauty*. Plants and flowers are universally acknowledged, as the most graceful and lovely objects, among the productions of nature. How charming is the variety, by which they are characterised! Some delight the eye with their rich tints, some with the delicate paleness of their hue, some with the grace and symmetry of their form, while all, without exception, testify, that the God of nature designed them to minister to man's delight, and to beautify the earth. Yet, whatever loveliness may appear in the productions of nature, but faintly shadows forth the beauty and glory of Him, by whom, and for whom, all things were created, and through whom all things consist. Jesus "is the chiefest among ten thousand, and altogether lovely," "fairer than the children of men," unspeakably eminent above every created being, in all that can command our esteem or excite our affection.

When, for us men, and for our salvation, He condescended to be planted in the unkindly soil, and under the unfavourable climate of this earth, the great mass of the Jews saw in Him "no form nor comeliness, nor any beauty, for which He was to be desired;" but those, from whose eyes the veil of prejudice and unbelief had been removed, "beheld His glory—the glory as of the only begotten of the Father, full of grace and truth." And so is it with men, at the present hour. To multitudes, His beauty is invisible; their carnal eyes cannot discern it. Destitute of true faith in Him, they have no realising, affecting views of His infinite excellency. The god of this world hath blinded their minds, lest the light of His glorious gospel should shine into them. True believers, on the other hand, "behold the beauty of the Lord;" for the eyes of their understanding have been opened, God having shined into their hearts, to give them the light of the knowledge of His glory in the face of Jesus Christ. Thus divinely illumined, even now they regard Him as unrivalled in brightness and beauty; and hereafter, they shall find their eternal happiness, in enjoying the fulfilment of the promise, "Thine eyes shall see the King in His beauty."

This celestial Plant is renowned for its *fragrance*. Some plants and flowers, which are justly celebrated on account of their pre-eminent beauty, are least distinguished for fragrance. There are others, however, which possess both these properties in a superior degree; for, while attracting our admiring gaze, they at the same time delight us with their sweet perfume. Even in our own climate, we can well appreciate the delicious fragrance, with which the sweet-smelling plants and flowers fill the atmosphere, throughout the summer months—

> "When, 'stead of one unchanging breeze,
> There blow a thousand gentle airs,
> And each a different perfume bears;
> As if the loveliest plants and trees
> Had vassal breezes of their own,
> To watch and wait on them alone,
> And waft no other breath than theirs."

But, in the sunnier climes of the East, such is the profusion of odoriferous plants, in some places, that we, in these northern climes, can form scarcely anything like an accurate idea of the delightful fragrance exhaled from them. Thus, the cedar trees and aromatic herbs, with which Lebanon abounds, send forth such a rich and powerful scent, that, even at a considerable distance, the atmosphere is redolent with the most grateful perfume. Accordingly, mention is made in Scripture of "the smell of Lebanon." But the sweetest fragrance of the choicest plants and flowers falls infinitely short of that, with which the Plant of Renown refreshes and delights the believer's soul. The very name of Jesus is "as ointment poured forth." "God hath anointed him with the oil of gladness above his fellows." "All his garments smell of myrrh, and aloes, and cassia, out of the ivory palaces." It is thus, too, that the Church describes His spiritual fragrance:—"Who is this that cometh out of the wilderness, like pillars of smoke, perfumed with myrrh and frankincense, with all powders of the merchant?" "A bundle of myrrh is my beloved unto me;" "He is like a cluster of camphire in the vineyards of Engedi." This celestial Plant has a delightful fragrance, even in the estimation of the eternal Father; for Christ's sacrifice is spoken of, as having "a sweet-smelling savour." His fragrance delights the hosts of heaven, among whom He now dwells; for His glorious name sounds from all their harps, and His love is the theme of their everlasting song. And to His people here on earth, incomparably more delightful is the contemplation of His work and character, than is the fragrance of the most favoured spot on earth to those who are faint and weary. Jesus is the Plant,

> "Whose holy fragrance fills the sky
> With balm of peace eternally."

This celestial Plant is renowned for its *healing virtues.* Some plants are in high repute, on account of their medicinal qualities. As an instance of this, the Balm of Gilead will at once occur to the mind of the reader. This was a sort of gum that exuded from the balsam-tree when pierced, and which was deemed of sovereign virtue, in healing the bites of serpents, and other dangerous wounds. But no plant possesses such a healing efficacy, as that which flows from the pierced and bleeding victim of a world's transgressions. The blood, which Jesus shed on Calvary, is better than medicine. It "ministers to minds diseased," and is a sovereign remedy for every wound and malady of the soul. When applied by the Holy Spirit to the conscience, and reccived by faith, it is able to restore soundness to those, who are sick even unto death. It mollifies and binds up the wounds of the broken-hearted, strengthens the weak, confirms the strong, opens the eyes of the blind, melts and subdues the stubborn and the obstinate, makes the dumb to sing, and causes the spiritually lame to run in the paths of God's commandments.

Nor is it only to the souls of true Christians, that this celestial Plant extends its sanative virtue. Its leaves are "for the healing of the nations," and its health-restoring efficacy is distinctly visible, even in the unregenerate world. It has produced a marvellous renovation, in the aspect and institutions of society. It has swept away the horrid abominations of heathenism, mitigated the ferocity of war, purified the tone of public morals, and refined the domestic affections. It has broken the fetters of the slave, and prompted to the formation of every institution, that is calculated to alleviate or remove human wretchedness. Despised and rejected of men, this heavenly Plant has done more to ameliorate even the temporal condition of our race, than all political or scientific institutions.

This celestial Plant is renowned for its *shade.* Even in our own comparatively temperate clime, it is often most refreshing to the traveller, wearied with his journey in the heat of an autumnal day, to retire to the cool shade of a large and widely-spreading tree. And how much more must this be the case, in the tropical climate of the East, where the beams of a vertical sun fall with such intense ardour! But oh! how faint an image is this of the shelter and refreshment afforded by the shadow of the Plant of Renown. Jesus is to His people as the "shadow of a great rock in a weary land." He is "a strength to the needy in his distress, a refuge from the storm, a shadow from the heat, when the blast of the terrible ones is as a storm against the wall." Beneath this shadow, Christ "makes His flock to rest at noon." Here they are effectually screened from the scorching heat of Jehovah's wrath, and from the curse of "a fiery law." "There is now no condemnation to them that are in Christ Jesus." Not less secure are they, who sit down under His shadow, from the heat of outward trials and afflictions. Accordingly, we find the sweet singer of Israel exclaiming, "Thou art my hiding-place; thou shalt preserve me from trouble; thou shalt compass me about with songs of deliverance." "He that dwelleth in the secret place of the Most High shall abide under the shadow of the Almighty. I will say of the Lord, He is my refuge and my fortress." In sitting beneath the shadow of Jesus, there is not merely security, but also "great delight." "Believing," the Christian "rejoices with joy unspeakable and full of glory." Then, too, are the virtues and graces of the spiritual life revived and strengthened. "They that dwell under his shadow shall return; they shall revive as the corn, and grow as the vine: the scent thereof shall be as the wine of Lebanon."

Reader, "abide in Jesus." Beyond His shadow, you can never obtain either safety, or true repose. All other refuges are refuges of lies. Like the gourd of Jonah, they may afford you a short-lived comfort; but soon, alas! shall the fire of God's anger burn them up, "that it shall leave them neither root nor branch." How blessed, on the other hand, is the condition of those, who have made the Lord their refuge, even the Most High their habitation! "The Lord is their keeper: the Lord is their *shade* upon their right hand. The sun shall not smite them by day, nor the moon by night. The Lord shall preserve them from all evil: he shall preserve their soul. The Lord shall preserve their going out and their coming in, from this time forth, and even for evermore."

This celestial Plant is renowned for its wholesome and pleasant *fruit.* If it is a pleasant thing for the weary, sun-beaten traveller, to retire from the noonday heat, to the cool and refreshing shade of a verdant tree, diffusing fragrance around the spot where it is reared, how does it enhance his delight, when the tree is richly laden with wholesome and pleasant fruit, upon which he may freely make his repast! And even thus is it with the Plant of Renown. "My beloved," says the Church, "is as the apple-tree. I sat down under his shadow with great delight, and His fruit was sweet to my taste." Christ's fruits, or, in other words, the blessings of His great salvation, are alike "pleasant to the eyes," and "good for food," and "able also to make wise unto salvation." Time would fail us, were we to attempt to enumerate these precious blessings. Whatever men need, or desire, may be obtained freely from Jesus. In Him, there is pardon for the guilty, life for the dead, bread for the hungry, water for the thirsty, clothing for the naked, strength for the weak, liberty for the captive, illumination for the ignorant, peace for the miserable, and, from the beginning to the end, supplies of grace, more than adequate to every form of want, and peculiarity of condition. Such are the golden fruits, which hang in rich clusters on the Plant of Renown. Sweet, however, as these are to the taste of those who partake of them, they are but as the grapes of Eshcol, compared with the infinitely richer and more delicious clusters, that grow so luxuriantly in the vineyards of the Canaan above. There, it will be granted unto all believers "to eat of the tree of life which is in the midst of the Paradise of God." "And he shewed me a pure river of water of life, clear as crystal, proceeding out of the throne of God and of the Lamb. In the midst of the street of it, and on either side of the river, was there the tree of life, which bare twelve manner of fruits, and yielded her fruit every month: and the leaves of the tree were for the healing of the nations."

Reader, would you partake of the fruits of salvation, with which the Plant of Renown is so richly laden? You have but to put forth the hand of faith, and pluck them from its clustered boughs. Although now transplanted to the midst of the Upper Paradise, its branches extend downwards to the very hand and mouth of sinners here on earth. Nor let the number of your wants deter you from plucking its golden fruit. The supply is inexhaustible. Countless myriads, who have gone before you, have taken of it freely, to their souls' satisfaction; but still there is no diminution—still there is enough, and to spare. Come, then, sit down under the shadow of this Plant, eat of its fruit, and live for ever.

But, have you already, in blessed experience, found, that Christ's fruit is indeed sweet unto your taste? Let your bosom swell with emotions of liveliest gratitude and praise to the "Giver of every blessing," for His infinite goodness, in raising up for you this Plant of Renown. Be it yours, however, to abide under its shadow, and to commend it to such as are now despising and rejecting it, and going through all the trees of the wood seeking, but seeking, alas! in vain, for rest and satisfaction. Anticipate, also, the full enjoyment of the Tree of Life in the midst of the Paradise of God, where, by eating of its delicious fruit, and inhaling the sweet fragrance of its leaves, you shall live for ever, in the uninterrupted and eternal enjoyment of a blessedness, such as "eye hath not seen, nor ear heard, neither hath it entered into the heart of man to conceive."

"As odours, press'd in summer hours
  From summer's bloom, remain;
To soothe and comfort, till the flowers
  Of spring revive again:

"So, till 'the Rose of Sharon' bloom
  Once more the desert's pride,
We feed upon the rich perfume
  It yielded when it died.

"'In earthen vessels,' weak and frail,
  The heav'nly treasure lies;
Enriching every passing gale
  With fragrance of the skies,—

"Faint breathings of the blessed morn,
That Advent shall restore,
When Christ shall to His own return,
Nor ever leave them more."

MONSELL.

The Sun of Righteousness.

HOSEA vi. 3.

"Then shall we know, if we follow on to know the Lord: his going forth is prepared as the morning; and he shall come unto us as the rain, as the latter and former rain unto the earth."

Ps. lxxxiv. 11.

"For the Lord God is a sun and shield; the Lord will give grace and glory: no good thing will he withhold from them that walk uprightly."

MALACHI iv. 2.

"But unto you that fear my name shall the Sun of righteousness arise with healing in his wings."

JOHN viii. 12.

"I am the light of the world: he that followeth me shall not walk in darkness, but shall have the light of life."

JOHN xii. 46.

"I am come a light into the world, that whosoever believeth on me should not abide in darkness."

2 COR. iv. 6.

"For God, who commanded the light to shine out of darkness, hath shined in our hearts, to give the light of the knowledge of the glory of God in the face of Jesus Christ."

ISA. lviii. 8.

"Then shall thy light break forth as the morning, and thine health shall spring forth speedily; and thy righteousness shall go before thee: the glory of the Lord shall be thy rereward."

"Dayspring of eternity!
Dawn on us this morning-tide.
Light from Light's exhaustless sea,
Now no more Thy radiance hide,
But dispel with glorious might
All our night.

"Let the morning dew of love
On our sleeping conscience rain;
Gentle comfort from above
Flow through life's long parchèd plain;
Water daily us Thy flock
From the rock.

"Let the glow of love destroy
Cold obedience faintly given;
Wake our hearts to strength and joy
With the flushing eastern heaven;
Let us truly rise ere yet
Life hath set.

"Brightest Star of eastern skies,
Let that final morn appear,
When our bodies, too, shall rise
Free from all that pain'd them here,
Strong their joyful course to run
As the sun.

"To yon world be Thou our light,
O Thou glorious Sun of grace;
Lead us, through the tearful night,
To yon fair and blessed place,
Where to joy that never dies
We shall rise."

VON ROSENROTH. 1684.

THE SUN OF RIGHTEOUSNESS.

HOW peculiarly appropriate, how strikingly beautiful is this appellation of our Lord! The sun is the grandest and most glorious object in the visible creation, and is, therefore, the fittest emblem of Him, who is "the brightness of his Father's glory, and the express image of his person," and in whom, in all its transcendent grandeur, "dwelleth all the fulness of the Godhead bodily." But this figure is expressive, not merely of the Saviour's essential and uncreated glory, but also of the powerful and benign influences, which are derived from Him, as our Redeemer. Viewed in this aspect, it is the purpose of the present chapter to shew, that He is to the spiritual world, what the sun is to the natural world—the source of light, fertility, comfort, and health.

We remark, then, that Jesus is styled the

Sun of Righteousness, because He communicates *light* to mankind. As the material sun dispels the gloomy horrors of the night, and enlightens universal nature with his beams, so Christ, the Sun of Righteousness, removes the thick veil of ignorance and superstition, and illumines the moral world with His heavenly instructions. Previously to His arising on the soul, all is darkness and disorder. Hence the apostle describes the unconverted, as "walking in the vanity of their minds, having the understanding darkened, being alienated from the life of God, through the ignorance that is in them, because of the blindness of their heart." Such is the mournful condition of man by nature; he is shut out from everything which it is of the deepest importance for him to know and understand; he discerns not spiritual things; he is moving onwards to that eternal world, upon which he must sooner or later enter, without that guidance and comfort, which would be to him, as lights flung across his path; and is like one, who knoweth not whither he goeth, because the darkness hath blinded his eyes. Nor can this spiritual gloom ever be dispelled, until the Sun of

Righteousness arises upon the soul, and imparts to it His almighty and enlightening influences. Then those, who "were sometime darkness," are made "light in the Lord;" a celestial radiance is poured into the chambers of the soul, the eyes of the understanding are opened, the attention is fixed upon the sublime statements and revelations of the word of truth, and the soul, which erewhile presented the aspect of moral chaos and gloom, is converted into the radiance and beauty of noonday. Most justly, therefore, may that blessed Saviour be styled the Sun of Righteousness, who thus "gives light to them that sit in darkness and in the shadow of death, and guides their feet into the way of peace."

This metaphor intimates, also, that the Messiah conveys *life and fertility* to the moral world. The great luminary of the natural world is not only the fountain of light; it is also the instrumental cause of vitality. Without its quickening and fructifying influence, vain would be the labour and skill of the husbandman. In winter, when we enjoy its presence least, how dead and desolate is the aspect of nature! Sullen vapours obscure the sky; the fields are stripped of their verdure, and the woods of their foliage; and the God of nature "sendeth forth his commandment upon earth, and giveth snow like wool; he scattereth the hoar-frost like ashes; he casteth forth his ice like morsels." But, at the approach of the vernal sun, all nature begins to flourish again. "For, lo, the winter is past, the rain is over and gone; the flowers appear on the earth; the time of the singing of birds is come, and the voice of the turtle is heard in the land; the fig-tree putteth forth her green figs, and the vines with the tender grape give a good smell." Similar to this, though infinitely surpassing it in beneficial influence, is the rising of the Sun of Righteousness upon the moral world. Naturally, the soul is in a state of desolation and death. Utterly insensible to the value of heavenly and eternal things, it has no desire whatever after the ennobling employments, and the exalted pleasures of religion. But, when the Sun of Righteousness arises upon the soul, it is quickened from this state of spiritual death; and the incorruptible seed of the Word having been implanted within it, and watered by the dews of Divine grace, the virtues and graces of the Holy Spirit spring up and abound, the wilderness becomes as a fruitful field, and the desert soul is made like unto the garden of the Lord. Then does Jehovah fulfil His own gracious promise, "I will be as the dew unto Israel; he shall grow as the lily, and cast forth his roots as Lebanon. His branches shall spread, and his beauty shall be as the olive-tree, and his smell as Lebanon. They that dwell under his shadow shall return; they shall revive as the corn, and grow as the vine; the scent thereof shall be as the wine of Lebanon." How wonderful is the transformation, which is thus effected by the light of the Sun of Righteousness shining in the soul! Formerly, it was in a state of spiritual torpor and death; now, it is alive unto God. Formerly, it was barren as the flinty rock; now, it is a tree abounding in the fruits of righteousness, to the praise and glory of God.

This metaphor further intimates, that Jesus Christ imparts *comfort and joy* to the souls of men. The natural sun is the source of comfort, as well as of light and fertility. How cold and cheerless would be our lives, without its genial warmth and enlivening beams! And how delightful is it, after the darkness of midnight, to welcome the first rays of the morning sun, and to inhale the refreshing influences thereby dispensed! "Truly, the light is sweet, and a pleasant thing it is for the eyes to behold the sun." All nature exults under the exhilarating beams of the ruler of the day, "coming forth like a bridegroom from his chamber;" the feathered songsters of the groves raise their tuneful notes; the fields smile in beauty and plenty; and, re-invigorated and cheered by its influence, men go forth from their dwellings to renew their daily toil. Thus cheering and reviving are the effects of the Sun of Righteousness, when He arises upon the downcast and sorrowful soul. By the instrumentality of His Word, and through the operations of His Holy Spirit, He pours His rich and overflowing consolations into the wounded souls of His people, re-invigorating them, as by some sovereign and reviving balm, and filling them with new strength and fresh alacrity, for what yet remains of the course set before them. He causes light to arise unto them in darkness, nay, even when they sit in darkness, He is Himself a light unto them, comforting them under the burden of spiritual distress, supporting them amid all the griefs and sorrows of their earthly pilgrimage, cheering them on in the path of duty, and animating them to every coming labour. And when His light is thus shed upon their spirits, there is far greater gladness put into their hearts, than the men of the world experience, even when their corn and wine do most abound. This spiritual gladness may not, indeed, be imparted to them in equal measure; but such is its inestimable nature, that even the least degree of it, that may be vouchsafed, will prevent the soul from ever again seeking its chief happiness from the gratifications of sense and time. It for ever palls the taste to every sinful pleasure. "Whoso drinketh of this living water shall never thirst again." It is a joy, which the world can neither give, nor take away; a stranger doth not intermeddle with it; and it constitutes the pledge and the foretaste of those rivers of pleasure, and of that fulness of joy which are at God's right hand for evermore.

This metaphor suggests, also, that the

Messiah is the source of *health* to the moral world. As the beams and influences of the natural sun diffuse health and vigour throughout the vegetable kingdom, so the Sun of Righteousness arises on the soul, "with healing in his wings." By nature, it is pervaded by the disease of sin, which prostrates its strength, covers it with moral pollution, and threatens it with eternal death. But, when the healing influences of the Sun of Righteousness are imparted, that fearful disease is removed from it, slowly, indeed, but surely; its energy is gradually restored; it is adorned with the beauties of holiness, and prepared for being translated into a region, the inhabitants of which "shall not say, I am sick," because they are "forgiven their iniquity,"—a region whence sin and temptation are for ever excluded, and where the saints of the Most High exist in undecaying youth, in unfading beauty, and in everlasting felicity. How great soever may be the defilement of the soul, to which His influences are conveyed, He is both able and willing to wash it all away. There is no case so desperate, that He cannot bring it to a favourable issue. "Though our sins be as scarlet, they shall be white as snow; though they be red like crimson, they shall be as wool."

Reader, are you still sitting in darkness, and in the region and shadow of death? Bethink you, how inexcusable and dangerous is your condition. Through the tender mercy of God, the Dayspring from on high hath visited you, and its light shines around you in meridian splendour. But this is your condemnation, that you love the darkness rather than the light, your deeds being evil. And if you continue thus to shut out the light of the Sun of Righteousness from your soul, your present darkness will inevitably become more dense and impenetrable, and prove but the forerunner of "the blackness of darkness for ever." Pray, then, earnestly and importunately, that "God, who at first commanded the light to shine out of darkness, may shine into your soul, to give you the light of the knowledge of His glory in the face of Jesus Christ." Break up your fallow ground, sow to yourself in righteousness, and open your heart to the benign influences of the Sun of Righteousness, while He is willing to communicate them. Follow Him, who declared Himself to be "the light of the world," and you "shall not walk in darkness, but shall have the light of life;" you shall enjoy all the blessings of His salvation,—the knowledge, the peace, the holiness, the felicity, which He, and He alone, can bestow.

But have the renovating influences of this blessed Luminary been imparted to your soul? "Blessed art thou of the Most High!" "You are the child of light, and of the day; you are not of the night, nor of darkness: therefore, sleep not, as do others, but watch and be sober; for they that sleep, sleep in the night, and they that be drunken, are drunken in the night. But you who are of the day, be sober; putting on the breastplate of faith and love, and for an helmet, the hope of salvation; for God hath not appointed you to wrath, but to obtain salvation by our Lord Jesus Christ." Let your path in faith, and purity, and love, be "as the morning light, which shineth more and more unto the perfect day." The firmament of your existence may frequently be overspread with clouds, and "for a season, if need be," you may be "in heaviness, through manifold temptations." But let not these things move you. Upon the darkest clouds of sorrow, the Sun of Righteousness shall shed a softening and a cheering light; and soon the day shall break, and the shades be dispelled. "Weeping may endure for a night, but joy cometh in the morning." Then, having come forth from the gloomy prison-house of death, you shall be ushered into a bright and glorious world, where no cloud ever darkens the sky, no chilling blast ever desolates the soil, but bright and serene day shines on perpetually, where "one unbounded spring encircles all," and the "storms of wintry Time" shall be felt no more. Raise, then, your thoughts to that celestial world,

"Where Christ, the Sun of Righteousness, displays
His beauteous form, with holy, matchless rays;
There His full presence, clear to ev'ry sight,
Fills every breast with exquisite delight."

"Though sunless, moonless, starless, seem
Each sufferer's lonely state,
There is a light whose cheering beam
Its gloom can dissipate;
It comes with healing in its wings,
And heav'nly radiance round it flings

"It rises on the darken'd mind
With lustre brighter far

Than that to outward orb assign'd,
 Of sun, or moon, or star;
And matchless in its mild control
 Over the desolate in soul."

BARTON

"Sun of my soul! Thou Saviour dear,
It is not night if Thou be near;
Oh! may no earth-born cloud arise
To hide Thee from Thy servant's eyes."

KEBLE.

"Suns may rise and suns may set,
 Summers come and summers go,
Earth its wintry grave forget,
 When the vernal breezes blow.

"But the day would be as night,
 And the summer winter prove,
If the rising of Thy light
 Did not wake our souls to love.

"Oh the blessedness of those
 Who Thine inner sunshine feel,
With its calm and soft repose,
 Gently o'er their spirits steal;

Who, as earth doth own the power
 Of her sun her life to wake,
Burst, as doth an opening flower,
 Into life for Jesus' sake

MONSELL.

The True Manna.

Ps. xxxiv. 8.

"O taste and see that the Lord is good: blessed is the man that trusteth in him."

Ps. xxxvi. 8.

"They shall be abundantly satisfied with the fatness of thy house; and thou shalt make them drink of the river of thy pleasures."

Ps. cxix. 103.

"How sweet are thy words unto my taste! yea, sweeter than honey to my mouth!"

Isa. lv. 1, 2, 3.

"Ho, every one that thirsteth, come ye to the waters, and he that hath no money: come ye, buy, and eat; yea, come, buy wine and milk without money, and without price. Wherefore do ye spend money for that which is not bread? and your labour for that which satisfieth not? hearken diligently unto me, and eat ye that which is good, and let your soul delight itself in fatness. Incline your ear, and come unto me: hear, and your soul shall live; and I will make an everlasting covenant with you, even the sure mercies of David."

John vi. 51.

"I am the living bread which came down from heaven: if any man eat of this bread, he shall live for ever: and the bread that I will give is my flesh, which I will give for the life of the world."

Rev. ii. 17.

"To him that overcometh will I give to eat of the hidden manna, and will give him a white stone, and in the stone a new name written, which no man knoweth saving he that receiveth it."

"Jesus, Thou art the living bread
By which our needy souls are fed;
In Thee alone Thy children find
Enough to fill the empty mind.

"Without this bread, I starve and die;
No other can my need supply;
But this will suit my wretched case,
Abroad, at home, in ev'ry place.

"'Tis this relieves the hungry poor,
Who ask for bread at mercy's door;
This living food descends from heav'n
As manna to the Jews was giv'n.

"This precious food my heart revives;
What strength, what nourishment it gives!
Oh, let me evermore be fed
With this divine, celestial bread."

FAWCETT.

THE TRUE MANNA.

MANY of those events, which happened under the Old Testament dispensation, undoubtedly bore a typical character. Of this description was the incident from which the title of the present chapter is borrowed. It appears that, about a month after the departure of the Israelites from Egypt, the provisions which they had brought with them having been exhausted, the whole congregation murmured against Moses and Aaron. In their sinful want of confidence in God, they had forgotten the galling and degrading servitude, from which they had been delivered, and ungratefully overlooked the miraculous interpositions, which they had experienced. But He, who had chosen them for His people, and placed them under His own special guardianship, had compassion on them though rebellious; and in order to silence their complaints, He "commanded the clouds from above, and opened the doors of heaven, and rained down manna upon them to eat, and gave them of the corn of heaven. Man did eat angels' food; he sent them meat to the full."

That this miraculous provision was designed to be an emblem of the Lord Jesus Christ, and of those precious blessings of which He is the Author, is evident from His own declaration, "I am the living bread which came down from heaven; if any man eat of this bread, he shall live for ever; and the bread that I will give is my flesh, which I will give for the life of the world." To the same effect is the testimony of St Paul, who, in writing to the Corinthians, declares, concerning the fathers under the Mosaic dispensation, that "they did all eat the same *spiritual meat.*" Authorised, then, by Christ Himself and by His apostle, let us follow out the emblem, and see the light which it sheds upon the character and work of Him who is the True Manna.

The manna in the wilderness *fell from heaven when the Israelites were ready to perish with hunger.* Even so Jesus descended from the heaven of heavens, where He had dwelt with the Father from the ages of eternity, in order to save "our souls alive"—to preserve them from that eternal decay, which, through sin, would otherwise have been their portion, and to nourish them to life eternal. The manna could, indeed, but faintly and imperfectly prefigure the "unspeakable gift" of God. For, instead of "angels' food," God hath given us the Lord and King of angels, and that, too, when our condition was far more desperate, than that of the Israelites in the desert. In consequence of his grievous and unprovoked rebellion, man had been cast out from the house of his heavenly Father, as unworthy even to eat of the crumbs which fell from His table; he had become "wretched, and miserable, and poor, and blind, and naked;" and, had he not obtained deliverance from this state of penury and destitution, he would inevitably have sunk at last into all the horrors of "the second death." But, while he was thus "without hope in the world," God looked upon him in mercy; and, to meet the distressing wants of his spiritual nature, He was pleased to send him the true bread from heaven, to whom whosoever cometh shall never hunger, and in whom whosoever believeth shall never thirst.

The manna *descended freely* around the tents of the murmuring Israelites; and, in like manner, the blessings of salvation through Christ are offered freely in the gospel. "By grace are ye saved, through faith, and that not of yourselves, it is the gift of God; not of works, lest any man should boast." The gospel salvation is no less freely offered, than it is provided. It is a gift, for which no price is demanded, and which looks for nothing in its recipient, but want and misery. Though unspeakably precious, it is placed within the reach of all; and, if we only ask in faith, it will be made ours. Sometimes men imagine, that their sins are too numerous, too aggravated, too enormous, to come to the Saviour; but not one is excluded. The vilest and most guilty criminals are as welcome to participate in the blessings of His salvation, as the most eminent saints. It is a feast, which He hath prepared for all men of every country, age, and condition; and the invitations to partake of it are no less unlimited. "Go ye," he said, "into all the world, and preach the gospel to every creature." "Ho, every one that thirsteth, come ye to the waters, and he that hath no money; come ye, buy and eat; yea, come, buy wine and milk, without money and without price." "Whosoever shall call upon the name of the Lord, shall be saved." Christ's provision for the need of sinners, is thus as unrestrictedly free to us, as the manna in the wilderness was to Israel. Those, therefore, who refuse or neglect to partake of it, are entirely without excuse.

The manna was *suitable alike to all*; and so the blessings of Christ's purchase are precisely such as are suited to the circumstances of His people. In their natural condition, they are hungering and thirsting after true happiness; but nothing in the wide range of the universe can ever satisfy the cravings of their immortal spirits. In regard to every object of earthly pursuit, it may be said, in the words of Solomon, that "the eye is not satisfied with seeing, nor the ear filled with hearing," and that "the appetite is not filled." But that satisfaction, which all created objects are unable to yield, is to be found in Jesus Christ. "He that cometh to me," He declares, "shall never hunger; and he that believeth on me shall never thirst." To all who are enlightened to know their own salvation, and are made acquainted with their own spiritual poverty, His salvation is "meat indeed, and drink indeed." How diversified soever their circumstances, they find in Him that spiritual nutriment, which is fitted to satisfy the largest wishes of their souls. Are they guilty? "In him they have redemption through his blood, the forgiveness of sins, according to the riches of his grace." Are they estranged from God? They are "made accepted in the beloved." Are they polluted? "He gave himself for them, that he might redeem them from all iniquity, and purify them unto himself a peculiar people, zealous of good works." Do enemies environ them on every side? His name is to them as "a strong tower, and rock of defence;" and He will enable them to retire from the field of conflict "more than conquerors." Do they need peace of heart? His dying legacy runs thus:—"Peace I leave with you, my peace I give unto you; not as the world giveth, give I unto you." Are they doomed to die, and to moulder away into dust? He is "the resurrection and the life," and hath promised to "redeem them from death, and ransom them from the power of the grave." As guilty and rebellious, are they in danger of the "second death?" He "delivereth them from the wrath to come," and "gives unto them eternal life, and they shall never perish, neither shall any one pluck them out of his hand." It is evident, then, that He, who is thus able to make "all grace to abound towards us," is precisely the kind of Saviour which our circumstances require. He is the true Bread of life, by which all who hunger and thirst after righteousness shall be filled.

It was necessary for the Israelites to *gather* the manna, though freely given of God; and, in like manner, it is required of us, that we believe to the saving of our souls. The mere knowledge of the fact, that Christ gave His flesh for the life of the world, can never of itself obtain for us a personal interest in His salvation. In order to this, we must receive Him by faith, as the food of our souls. His own declaration is, "Verily, verily, I say unto you, except ye eat the flesh of the Son of man, and drink his blood, ye have no life in you."

Nor is the faith, by which we obtain a personal interest in Christ and His salvation, a mere transient and solitary act. As the Israelites gathered the manna *daily*, even so must we be daily feeding upon the heavenly bread offered to us in the gospel. Our whole life, in fact, must be a life of faith upon the Son of God. And how encouraging the thought, that we may always have the grace that we need. For "thus saith the Lord that created the heavens, I said not unto the seed of Jacob, Seek ye me in vain." "I will make an everlasting covenant with them, that I will not turn away from them to do them good; but I will put my fear in their hearts, that they shall not depart from me." Upon Christ, then, let us feed daily and hourly; upon His promised grace and strength be it ours to live all the day long; while, in all time of our want and weakness, let our language be like his of old—"In the Lord have I righteousness and strength."

As the manna *sustained* the Israelites from day to day, so are they supported and strengthened who live by faith upon the Son of God. They dwell in Him, and He dwells in them; and in consequence of this mysterious union, that spiritual life which they receive from Him is maintained and strengthened, as He Himself tells us, saying, "As the living Father hath sent me, and I live by the Father, even so he that eateth me shall live by me." Hence He declares, "Whoso eateth my flesh, and drinketh my blood, hath eternal life; and I will raise him up at the last day." By union with Him, believers obtain that spiritual nourishment and strength whereby they are enabled to make progress in their journey to the celestial Canaan. Eating of the living bread, ofttimes do they find that, like Elijah the prophet, they are borne up under the fatigues and sufferings of the wilderness, and go in the strength of that meal many days. Nay, such is its transcendent efficacy, that it will crown them with life eternal beyond death and the grave. "He that eateth of this bread shall live for ever."

The appointed mode of *distributing* the manna among the Israelites is not without its significance. Some gathered more, and others less; but all received a plentiful supply. So believers receive liberally out of the "exceeding abundant grace of Christ."

"It pleased the Father, that in him should all fulness dwell;" and if we only come to Him, we shall receive, "out of his fulness, grace for grace," abundance of every kind of heavenly and spiritual blessings. If we are hungering and thirsting, it is not because He is either unable or unwilling to satisfy our wants, but solely because we, being "of little faith," do not come to Him, "that we may have life, and that we may have it more abundantly." The cause of our being straitened is in ourselves, and not in our Lord, who is "the only-begotten of the Father, full of grace and truth," and who hath promised to every believer, "Open thy mouth wide, and I will fill it."

And as the Israelites were required freely to *impart* of their manna to those who had lack, so we are commanded to make known the gospel to all. Freely having received, it is incumbent upon us freely to give; and if we selfishly hoard up the bread of life, and thus disobey the heavenly injunction to distribute it to those, who are perishing for lack of knowledge, we have but too much reason to fear that we ourselves have never yet come to Christ, and been made partakers of His flesh.

As the manna was, at a subsequent stage in their journeyings, *rejected* by the Israelites, so was Christ despised and rejected by them as a nation, and is now lightly esteemed by thousands whom He invites to come unto Him. "Our soul loatheth this light bread," said the Israelites in the desert; and in like manner it has been said by multitudes who are ignorant of their own spiritual wants, "We will not have this man to reign over us."

A portion of the manna was *laid up* in the golden vessels of the tabernacle, where it remained for ages without suffering corruption. Even so, Jesus Christ liveth for ever in the heavenly sanctuary, as "the hidden manna," which He promises for the support and nourishment of His conflicting and overcoming people. And as He is represented in Holy Writ as dwelling in our hearts by faith, may not the purity of the golden vessels in which the manna was preserved as a memorial, teach us to cleanse our hearts from all sin and corruption, that they may be fit receptacles for Jesus Christ, the True Manna?

But, while the manna in the wilderness thus furnishes an apt illustration of Christ, and His salvation, it must be remembered, that, in some important respects, this illustration is defective. It has been truly remarked, indeed, that "the brightest type is dim beside the glory of His person and work."

The manna was restricted to the Israelites themselves; but Christ is free both to Jews and Gentiles. He gave His flesh for the life of the world,—for the salvation of mankind of every kindred, people, and nation. Wherever death and sin have extended, there the remedy is provided. "As in Adam all die, so in Christ shall many be made alive."

The manna could only feed the bodies of the Israelites, and could not preserve them from death at last. "Your fathers did eat manna in the wilderness, and are dead," was the language of Christ to their descendants. "But this," said He of Himself, "is the bread which cometh down from heaven, that a man may eat thereof, and not die." This heavenly bread preserves all who partake of it from "the second death," and communicates and sustains a spiritual and eternal life.

The manna fell only while the Israelites

were in the wilderness, and ceased when they entered the land of Canaan; but this mystical bread continueth for ever, and is most fully enjoyed in the Canaan above, where all wants are supplied, and all wishes gratified,—where the inhabitants "hunger no more, neither thirst any more, neither doth the sun light on them nor any heat, but the Lamb who is in the midst of the throne feeds them and leads them unto living fountains of waters, and God wipes away all tears from their eyes."

Reader, be this your earnest and daily prayer, "Lord, evermore give me this Bread!"

"Bread of the world, in mercy broken!
Wine of the soul, in mercy shed!
By whom the words of life were spoken,
And in whose death our sins are dead!

"Look on the heart by sorrow broken,
Look on the tears by sinners shed;
And be Thy feast to us the token,
That by Thy grace our souls are fed."

HEBER.

"And art Thou ready, Saviour dear,
And is Thy table spread for me?
But the poor soul that should draw near
Still all unreadiness for Thee?

"Hast Thou come down, with tender care
Thy weary people's hearts to bless,
And host, and feast,—dost Thou prepare
A table in the wilderness?

"And still, can dying souls refuse
To take the bliss while yet they may;
With some poor plea their sin excuse,
And, cold and heartless, turn away?

'Teach me, O God, 'the better part,'
When I some vain excuse would plead;
What stills not my own anxious heart,
How could it e'er with Thee succeed?

"Or if the joys bestow'd on earth
Shine only to distract from heav'n,
Not only are they little worth,
But better they had ne'er been giv'n."

MONSELL.

The Smitten Rock.

DEUT. xxxii. 31.

"For their rock is not as our Rock, even our enemies themselves being judges."

PS. lxi. 2.

"From the end of the earth will I cry unto thee, when my heart is overwhelmed: lead me to the Rock that is higher than I."

ISA. xli. 17, 18.

"When the poor and needy seek water, and there is none, and their tongue faileth for thirst, I the Lord will hear them, I the God of Israel will not forsake them. I will open rivers in high places, and fountains in the midst of the valleys: I will make the wilderness a pool of water, and the dry land springs of water."

ISA. xliii. 20.

"The beast of the field shall honour me, the dragons and the owls: because I give waters in the wilderness, and rivers in the desert, to give drink to my people, my chosen."

EZEK. xxxvi. 25.

"Then will I sprinkle clean water upon you, and ye shall be clean: from all your filthiness, and from all your idols, will I cleanse you."

JOHN vii. 37, 38.

"In the last day, that great day of the feast, Jesus stood and cried, saying, If any man thirst, let him come unto me, and drink. He that believeth on me, as the Scripture hath said, out of his belly shall flow rivers of living water."

1 COR. x. 4.

"And did all drink the same spiritual drink; for they drank of that spiritual rock that followed them; and that rock was Christ."

REV. xxi. 6.

"I will give unto him that is athirst of the fountain of the water of life freely."

"Rock of ages! cleft for me,
Let me hide myself in Thee!
Let the water and the blood,
From Thy wounded side that flow'd,
Be of sin the double cure;
Cleanse me from its guilt and power.

"Not the labour of my hands
Can fulfil Thy law's demands;
Could my zeal no respite know—
Could my tears for ever flow,—
All for sin could not atone;
Thou must save, and Thou alone.

"Nothing in my hand I bring,
Simply to Thy cross I cling;
Naked, come to Thee for dress;
Helpless, look to Thee for grace;
Vile, I to the fountain fly—
Wash me. Saviour, or I die!

"While I draw this fleeting breath;
When my eyelids close in death;
When I soar to worlds unknown—
See Thee on Thy judgment throne
Rock of ages cleft for me,
Let me hide myself in Thee."

THE SMITTEN ROCK.

SOON after the children of Israel experienced the miraculous interposition referred to in the preceding chapter, they encamped at a place called Rephidim, where, the sacred historian informs us, "there was no water for the people to drink." Notwithstanding the many signal deliverances which they had experienced on former occasions, no sooner were they exposed to this additional privation, than they relapsed into unbelief, and renewed their complaints and murmurings. Agitated by impatience, they not only chidingly demanded water of Moses, but accused him of having brought them out of Egypt, to kill them, and their children, and their cattle with thirst. Nay, to such an outrageous extent did they vent their unhallowed feelings, that they actually threatened to stone him to death.

In these most distressing circumstances, Moses cried unto the Lord, and in answer to his prayer, was informed as to the mode in which the wants of the people were to be relieved. Attended by some of the elders of Israel, and having in his hand the wonder-working rod, wherewith he had smitten the river, Moses was to go on before the people to Horeb, where he was to smite a rock, from which copious streams of water should gush out. "And Moses did so in the sight of the elders of Israel." "He opened the rock, and the waters gushed out; they ran in the dry places like a river."

That this memorable incident was designed to be emblematic of the Lord Jesus Christ, and the blessings of His salvation, appears from the language of St Paul, in his first epistle to the Corinthians, where he says, "they drank of that spiritual rock that followed them, and that rock was Christ." In the present chapter, therefore, it is purposed to indicate a few of the leading correspondences between the rock, which on this occasion supplied the thirsty multitude with water, and that which it prefigured.

The rock at Horeb suggests the ideas of

stability and unchangeableness. As it has withstood the storms of centuries, it serves to illustrate, in some faint degree, the everlasting existence and immutability of Him who is the "Rock of ages." Before the mountains were brought forth, He was in the bosom of the Father. He "was set up from everlasting, from the beginning, or ever the earth was. When there were no depths, he was brought forth; when there were no fountains abounding with water, he was by God, as one brought up with him, and he was daily his delight, rejoicing always before him." And as He had no "beginning of days," so neither shall He have any "end of life." Hence, He is described by an apostle, as "the same yesterday, to-day, and for ever."

How admirably fitted is this truth to support and comfort the believer, amid all the vicissitudes and trials of time! The whole scenery of life is continually shifting around us. The fashion of the world passeth away. Generation succeedeth generation, as wave succeedeth wave. "The memory of man passeth away, like the remembrance of a guest who hath tarried but one night." Brief as is our sojourn here below, by how many changes is it distinguished! It affords us nothing on which we can set up our rest, no possession or enjoyment which we can properly call our own. When our mountain seems to stand strong, and our hearts are fondly indulging the anticipation, that the fabric of bliss which we have reared shall always endure, not seldom does some unexpected and unprepared-for shock descend, and, in one short hour, leave us to mourn, in sadness and dismay, over the wrecks and fragments of what we once deemed precious. Our health declines, our friends are taken from us, the gourd of our prosperity is blasted, our hopes are blighted, some event or another is not long of occurring to convince us of the uncertainty and transitoriness of everything worldly—that "time and chance happen alike to all," and that "all is vanity and vexation of spirit." Amidst all these sorrows and changes, how consoling and animating is the thought, that He, to whom the believer has intrusted his eternal safety, never changes, and can never die! He can never cease to be what He is, and always has been. "I am" is His name, and His memorial to all generations. All created things may be shadowy, and fleeting, and vain; but the Rock of ages is immovable, and therefore the sons of men may abide in safety and peace under His shadow. Oh! let us "trust in the Lord for ever, for in the Lord Jehovah is everlasting strength."

The rock which supplied the Israelites with water was *chosen by God himself.* It is evident that He might easily have supplied their wants in various other ways, than by causing the water to flow out of a barren and flinty rock. He might have commanded the heavens to give forth their rain, or conducted His people to another Elim, "where were twelve wells of water, and threescore and ten palm trees." Nay, He could have provided as plentiful a supply for His distressed people, by causing the waters to gush out of the hot and arid sands beneath their very feet. But, with the view of asserting His sovereignty, He pointed out to His servant Moses this particular rock, and commanded him, in the employment of certain appointed means, to seek for water there. "The Lord said unto Moses, Go on before the people, and take with thee of the elders of Israel: and thy rod, wherewith thou smotest the river, take in thine hand, and go. Behold, I will stand before thee there upon the rock in Horeb, and thou shalt smite the rock, and there shall water come out of it, that the people may drink." So, in like manner, did God appoint His own Son to be a High-Priest and Mediator. "He laid help upon one that is mighty: he exalted one chosen out of the people." "The Lord hath *laid on him*, (that is, Christ,) the iniquity of us all."

This divine selection of Christ to be the Saviour of sinners may well inspire all who believe in Him with confidence and hope; for He will in no wise cast out those who come to Him in the way of His own appointment. On the other hand, it is equally clear, that all, who seek salvation in any other way, must inevitably come short of it; for, as the water was to issue only from the particular rock which was chosen of God, so in vain do we expect salvation from any save Him who "verily was fore-ordained before the foundation of the world." He is "God, and there is none else." "Other foundation can no man lay than that which is laid, even Jesus Christ." "There is none other name under heaven given among men whereby we must be saved."

Ere the waters proceeded from the rock at Horeb, it was, by God's appointment, *smitten by the rod of Moses.* So Jesus Christ, as the source of all spiritual blessings to the world, was "smitten, stricken of God, and afflicted," according as Jehovah, by His servant Zechariah, had predicted,—"Awake, O sword, against my shepherd, and against the man that is my fellow, saith the Lord of hosts; *smite* the shepherd, and the sheep shall be scattered: and I will turn mine hand upon the little ones." How literally was this ancient oracle fulfilled in those unspeakable sufferings to which Jesus was exposed by the appointment of His Father! When "He was taken from prison, and from judgment, and as a lamb was led to the slaughter," His sacred body was smitten, and mangled, and pierced, till "His visage became more marred than any man's, and His form more than the sons of men!" Nor was it in His body alone, that He was smitten: "the iron entered into His soul." Accordingly, we find Him, in the extremity of His anguish, exclaiming, "My soul is exceeding sorrowful, even unto death." "Now is my soul troubled; and what shall I say? Father, save me from this hour: but for this cause came I unto this hour."

It is impossible, indeed, to conceive the unparalleled intensity of His sufferings. Never was "any sorrow like unto His sorrow, which was done unto Him, wherewith the Lord had afflicted Him, in the day of His fierce anger." As to the *cause* of these sufferings, however, we are not left in ignorance or doubt. It is plainly revealed to us in the gospel of His grace, that they were *vicarious* and *expiatory* in their character. "He bore our sins on his own body on the tree." "He was wounded for our transgressions, he was bruised for our iniquities; the chastisement of our peace was upon him: and with his stripes we are healed." It was because we had violated God's holy law, and trampled under foot the authority of His moral government, that it became necessary for Him to interpose in our behalf; and, in his infinite mercy and love, He endured the penalty that was due to our transgressions. He placed Himself in our room and stead. He interposed His sacred person between us and the vengeance of heaven; and because that person was divine no less than human,

He was enabled to bear the stroke of that mighty vengeance, and to make honourable the holy law of God, which had declared, "Cursed is every one that continueth not in all things which are written in the book of the law to do them." And now, "there is no condemnation to them that are in Christ Jesus, who walk not after the flesh, but after the Spirit;" for He hath "redeemed us from the curse of the law, being made a curse for us."

The waters that flowed from the smitten rock *saved the Israelites from perishing by thirst.* Had not this miraculous supply been obtained, the inevitable result must have been, that, overcome by thirst and fatigue, the whole multitude would have perished in the wilderness. And can we fail to perceive, in the painful privations to which they were now exposed, a striking emblem of the believer's condition in the "waste howling wilderness" of this world? By nature, he is exposed to the most pressing spiritual want, being, in consequence of his guilt and depravity, destitute of the favour of God, and of all true happiness; and, unless he obtain deliverance from this state, it will prove but the forerunner of everlasting sorrow. If he be pressed by a sense of his destitution, he can find nothing around him capable of satisfying the wants of his soul, or of inspiring it with true, solid, lasting peace. The world in all its forms is found a vain and unsatisfying portion. Disappointment meets him at every stage of his career. No sooner does he grasp those objects on which he had set his heart, than he finds that their dimensions are far too scanty to fill the soul—to satisfy the undying thirst within. The sense of want still remains, and he is compelled to acknowledge, that, in reference to the satisfaction and happiness of the soul, all that this earth can offer has been as yet to him but vanity and vexation of spirit.

When, however, he repairs in faith to Jesus Christ, the Rock of ages, he immediately finds that happiness, for which he had so earnestly longed in vain. Resting on that firm foundation, his soul is made happy in the favour and enjoyment of God. The aching void, which the world could never fill, is now replenished with a peace that passeth understanding, and with a joy that is unspeakable and full of glory. Not more gladly did the thirsty pilgrims at Rephidim hear the sound of the waters gushing from the smitten rock, than the sinner, ready to perish, hears the voice "of Him that bringeth good tidings, that publisheth peace, that bringeth good tidings of good, that publisheth salvation, that saith unto Zion, Thy God reigneth." God is now reconciled, and the assurance of pardon and acceptance is to the trembling penitent even as a spring of water to him who is athirst.

The waters that issued from the rock at Horeb served to *purify the Israelites from the defilements of the sandy wilderness.* Even so is it with the precious blood of Christ, which, as the apostle declares, "cleanseth us from all sin." It frees us not only from its *guilt*, but also from its *defilement.* It purchased the regenerating and sanctifying influences of the Holy Spirit, who "worketh effectually in them that believe." Had Christ, indeed, merely removed our guilt, only a part of His gracious object in coming into the world would have been attained. Enthralled by the fetters of sin, His people could never have advanced one single step, along the pilgrim path, that leads to heaven.

But, blessed be God! the salvation, which He hath wrought out for them, is, in every respect, suitable and complete. The Holy Spirit is promised to believers day by day; nay, He is described as an indwelling Spirit, carrying on the process of renovation in their hearts, subduing, purifying, and ennobling them, till at last they are made "meet for the inheritance of the saints in light." Hence, on account of its cleansing property, water is frequently used in Scripture to signify the sanctifying influences of the Spirit of Christ. Thus the prophet Zechariah, in foretelling the effects of His advent, says, "In that day there shall be a fountain opened for sin and for uncleanness." This celestial Fountain, like the pool at Bethesda, is able to make all, who wash in it, "whole of whatsoever disease they have." Being justified, they shall be also sanctified, "in the name of the Lord Jesus, and by the Spirit of our God." So long as they remain in this world, sin may indeed *exist*, but it does not *reign* in them; it may not be *destroyed*, but it is *subdued;* and they earnestly long for the period, when "the only wise God, their Saviour, shall present them faultless before the presence of His glory with exceeding joy."

The waters from the smitten rock *refreshed the Israelites*, when, "hungry and thirsty, their soul fainted in them." And is it not thus with the weary and heavy-laden traveller to Zion, when supplies from the Redeemer's grace are afforded to his soul? This world is to him but a cheerless and barren desert, amid the manifold fatigues and cares of which "his spirit often faileth; his spirit is overwhelmed within him; his heart within him is desolate." But when the graces and consolations of the Holy Spirit abound, then to him is "the wilderness and solitary place made glad, and the desert rejoices and blossoms as the rose." Having drunk of "the brook in the way," he again lifts up his head, and with renewed vigour and alacrity resumes his heavenward course.

And where, save in Jesus Christ, can we ever obtain that spiritual refreshment, which we need? It is not to be found in the world. All its pleasures, riches, and honours can never restore tranquillity to the troubled soul, and peace to the wounded spirit. They are unsatisfying, delusive, and vain—broken cisterns which can hold no water, no living water such as the soul desireth. Like the deceitful *mirage*, they disappoint all our expectations, and leave us as far as ever from the happiness which our souls long for. But it is not thus with the promises and consolations of the gospel. There, all is real, nothing is imaginary. There, the spirit obtains genuine consolation, and draws water with joy out of the well of life; there, its peace becomes as a river, and its righteousness as a flowing stream. And the felicity, which it enjoys on earth, is but the prelude and earnest of those overflowing pleasures, of which it is destined to partake in the paradise of God. "Whosoever drinketh," said Jesus, "of the water that I shall give him, shall never thirst; but the water that I shall give him, shall be in him a well of water springing up into everlasting life."

The waters from the opened rock were so *abundant, as to supply the whole camp of Israel*, and yet were not exhausted. So is it with the grace of our Lord Jesus Christ. It is, as St Paul declares, "exceeding abundant." Its efficacy to save, purify, and refresh our souls is inexhaustible. It is amply sufficient to meet the most pressing necessities of all who are partakers of it, whether Jew or Greek, barbarian or Scythian, bond or free. "In Christ all fulness dwells," so that, whatever men need or desire, He is "able to do unto them exceeding abundantly above all that they ask or think." The believer may be in want, but it will be because he does not ask. He can never be straitened in Christ: the fountain of His grace is inexhaustible, and the more widely its streams are diffused, the deeper do they become.

The waters from the rock were *accessible to all.* So is it with Christ's rich provision for the need of sinners. It is offered unto all, without respect of persons. As the rain descending alike on the evil and the good, as sunshine mantling in its glory the humble vale as well as the lofty mountain, the wilderness as well as the fertile field, the peasant's cottage as well as the noble's mansion,—so is the salvation of the gospel a common blessing. It is designed for the young, for the middle-aged, and for the old; for the rich, and for the poor, and for those to whom neither poverty nor riches have been given; for the prosperous and for the afflicted; for the happy and for the miserable; for the great and for the mean; for the savage and for the civilized; for the monarch and for the slave. In complete accordance with this view of the gospel salvation, the invitations to partake of it addressed to sinners in the Scriptures are impartial and free. "Ho, every one that thirsteth, come ye to the waters." "And the Spirit and the bride say, Come; and let him that heareth say, Come; and let him that is athirst come; and *whosoever will*, let him take the water of life *freely*."

The waters from the smitten rock flowed *constantly*. Neither the winter's frost nor the summer's drought could arrest their progress; but, like a river of many streams, coming from fountains that never fail, they continued to hold on their undiminished and majestic course, following the Israelites in all their desert wanderings, and daily supplying their wants, until they entered the Promised Land. Hence, in the passage already quoted from the First Epistle to the Corinthians, the apostle informs us, "They drank of that spiritual rock that *followed* them." So the mercy and grace of the Redeemer are never suspended in their exercise, but continue to flow for the refreshment and salvation of His people as they prosecute their heavenward course. The rills of creature comfort may be likened unto "the streams of brooks, which pass away. What time they wax warm, they vanish; when it is hot, they are consumed out of their place." But the fountain that was opened for sin and for uncleanness is one that never fails—one whose streams are ever flowing, ever full. In ages that are gone, countless myriads have repaired to it, and been satisfied with its divine consolations, and yet there is no diminution. Goodness and mercy still follow the true Israel of God, during all their earthly pilgrimage. Nothing can arrest the progress of that "river, whose streams make glad the city of our God, the holy place of the tabernacle of the Most High." Like a torrent swollen by the rain of heaven, it rushes onward, breaking down every opposing mound, sweeping before it every bulwark raised in order to prevent its progress, and forcing a way for itself into all the nations of the earth. "Living waters," saith the Lord, "shall go out from Jerusalem, half of them toward the former sea, and half of them toward the latter sea; in summer and in winter shall it be." Already has this gracious promise been largely fulfilled; and though Zion may occasionally be parched with drought, yet "times of refreshing shall come from the presence of the Lord." For "the Lord will comfort Zion, he will comfort her waste places, and he will make her wilderness like Eden, and her desert like the garden of the Lord."

Reader, how deep should be your gratitude to the Father of mercies and the God of all consolation, in that He hath so liberally provided for your wants in this dry and thirsty land. "Give thanks," then, "unto the Lord, for he is good, for his mercy endureth for ever." The waters of the river, which gladdens our Zion, are, through the Spirit, made more than adequate to every form of want, and peculiarity of condition. Under all your wanderings, they will never leave, nor forsake you; and while you drink of them, you have a foretaste of those "rivers of pleasures," which are at God's right hand for evermore. "Abide," therefore, "in Jesus." Day by day renew your application to Him, in whom "are all your springs." Beware of wandering from the "fountain of living waters," for, nowhere else, can you obtain true consolation and peace. All earthly pleasures are but "broken cisterns," and will leave the weary traveller, without comfort, and without hope, in the hour of his greatest need. Never, therefore, forsake the waters of the sanctuary for such pernicious and deadly streams; but habitually remember, and use your lofty privilege of access to Him, who alone is able to quench the thirst of your soul, and to refresh and invigorate you, at every stage of your wilderness journey.

But, if you are still at a distance from Christ, let me exhort you, as you value your immortal soul, to betake yourself to the fountain He hath opened, while access yet remains. Soon shall all those streams of false comfort, from which you now vainly seek to obtain satisfaction, be completely dried up, and it will be with every impenitent and unbelieving sinner, "as when a thirsty man dreameth, and behold, he drinketh, but he awaketh, and behold, he is faint, and his soul hath appetite." You will stand before the dread tribunal of Christ, and cry and pray for mercy there, but then it will be too late You shall be driven away from His presence, and consigned to that awful abode where "the worm dieth not, and the fire is not quenched," and where not a drop of water can be obtained to cool your tongue. Blessed be God! a door of hope is still open unto you. The gospel is now preached, and its blessings are freely offered, even to the chief of sinners. There is no depth of guilt and misery from which divine grace cannot deliver you; and there is no height of holiness and perfection to which it cannot elevate you. Thou hast fallen, O sinner, by thine iniquities, but God thine helper is great! But while there is salvation in Christ for all, remember that there is salvation in none other. If you do not believe in Christ, you must perish eternally. There is no expiation for sin but the atonement He has made; there is no saving interest in that atonement but through believing. If you do not drink of the water of life that is offered, your thirst remains. Comply, then, with Christ's merciful invitation, come unto Him, and drink. Then will He not only comfort and refresh you amid all your pilgrim toils and sufferings, but, in due time, conduct you, in safety and peace, to a city eternal habitation in the Canaan above.

"Ho, ye that pant for living streams,
And pine away and die,
Here you may quench your raging thirst
With springs that never dry.

"Rivers of love and mercy here
In a rich ocean join;
Salvation in abundance flows,
Like floods of milk and wine.

"Dear Lord, the treasures of Thy love
Are everlasting mines,
Deep as our helpless mis'ries are,
And boundless as our sins.

"The happy gates of gospel grace
Stand open night and day,
Lord, we are come to seek supplies,
And drive our wants away."

WATTS.

"This land through which His pilgrims go
Is desolate and dry;
But streams of grace from Him o'erflow,
Their thirst to satisfy.

"When troubles, like a burning sun,
Beat heavy on their head,
For shelter to this Rock they run,
And find a pleasant shade.

"How glorious he! how happy they
In such a glorious Friend!
Whose love secures them all the way,
And crowns them at the end!"

NEWTON.

"Bless'd Jesus, source of grace divine,
What soul-refreshing streams are Thine
Oh bring these healing waters nigh,
Or we must droop, and fall, and die.

"No traveller through desert lands,
'Midst scorching suns and burning sands,
More needs the current to obtain,
Or to enjoy refreshing rain.

"Our longing souls aloud would sing;
Spring up, celestial Fountain, spring!
To a redundant river flow,
And cheer this thirsty land below.

"May this bless'd torrent near my side
Through all the desert gently glide:
Then, in Emmanuel's land above,
Spread to a sea of joy and love!"

DODDRIDGE.

The Brazen Serpent.

JOHN iii. 14, 15.

"And as Moses lifted up the serpent in the wilderness, even so must the Son of man be lifted up: that whosoever believeth in him should not perish, but have eternal life."

JOHN xii. 32, 33.

"And I, if I be lifted up from the earth, will draw all men unto me. This he said, signifying what death he should die."

ISA. xlv. 22.

"Look unto me, and be ye saved, all the ends of the earth; for I am God, and there is none else."

ROM. iii. 24, 25, 26.

"Being justified freely by his grace, through the redemption that is in Christ Jesus; whom God hath set forth to be a propitiation through faith in his blood, to declare his righteousness for the remission of sins that are past, through the forbearance of God; to declare, I say, at this time his righteousness; that he might be just, and the justifier of him which believeth in Jesus."

EPH. ii. 8.

"For by grace are ye saved through faith; and that not of yourselves: it is the gift of God."

JOHN iii. 36.

"He that believeth on the Son hath everlasting life: and he that believeth not the Son shall not see life; but the wrath of God abideth on him."

"So did the Hebrew prophet raise
The brazen serpent high,
The wounded felt immediate ease,
The camp forbore to die.

"Look upwards in the dying hour,
'And live,' the prophet cries:
But Christ performs a nobler cure
When faith lifts up her eyes.

"High on the cross the Saviour hung,
High in the heavens He reigns:
Here sinners by th' old Serpent stung
Look, and forget their pains.

"When God's own Son is lifted up,
A dying world revives,
The Jew beholds the glorious hope,
Th' expiring Gentile lives."

WATTS

THE BRAZEN SERPENT.

IN the above title, there is an allusion to another miraculous deliverance, which was wrought for Israel in the wilderness. They were now journeying from Mount Hor, by the way of the Red Sea, and had arrived at the desolate region lying to the east of the mountains of Edom, where, we are told, "the soul of the people was much discouraged because of the way," and they renewed their murmurings against God, and against Moses, saying, "Wherefore have ye brought us up out of Egypt to die in the wilderness? for there is no bread, neither is there any water: and our soul loatheth this light bread." This conduct, so criminal in itself, and so inconsistent with the goodness they had experienced, and the privileges they enjoyed, provoked the displeasure of the Almighty, which was manifested by His sending fiery serpents among them, "which bit the people, and much people of Israel died." Agitated by alarm, they came to Moses, confessed their guilt, and besought him to intercede for them with their offended God. With this request Moses at once complied, and, in answer to his intercession, the Lord said unto him, "Make thee a fiery serpent, and set it upon a pole: and it shall come to pass, that every one that is bitten, when he looketh upon it shall live. And Moses made a serpent of brass, and put it upon a pole, and it came to pass, that if a serpent had bitten any man, when he beheld the serpent of brass, he lived."

It has sometimes been questioned whether this memorable incident was intended to be typical of the nature and effects of our Saviour's death. But it is, beyond all controversy, a fair illustration of them, and is applied as such by Himself, when He says, "As Moses lifted up the serpent in the wilderness, even so must the Son of man be lifted up: that whosoever believeth in Him should not perish, but have everlasting life." Again He declares, "I, if I be lifted up from the earth, will draw all men unto me." And the evangelist explains, that "this He said, signifying what death He should die." In the sequel of this chapter, therefore, it is purposed to point out some of the more prominent points of resemblance between the incident under consideration, and the atoning death of the Son of God.

The *lifting up* of the brazen serpent presents an evident illustration of Christ's crucifixion. The brazen serpent was set on a pole, and lifted up in a conspicuous part of the camp, that it might be seen by the whole congregation of Israel. Even so the Son of God was crucified in the most public manner at Jerusalem, on an eminence, amidst many thousands of tumultuous spectators. Moses lifted up the serpent, at the commandment of the Lord. In like manner Jesus Christ was lifted up on the cross, according to the divine appointment. The Lord laid on Him the iniquities of us all; and when, with wicked hands, the Jews crucified the Lord of glory, they fulfilled, though they knew it not, the divine purpose; they did nothing more than what the hand and counsel of Heaven had "determined before to be done."

The brazen serpent was lifted up, that *whosoever beheld it might be healed of their deadly wounds, and live.* So Christ was crucified, that whosoever believeth in Him might not perish, but have everlasting life. In consequence of our natural guilt and depravity, our condition is infinitely worse than that of the serpent-stung Israelites. For, while they were threatened only with the death of the *body*, our immortal *souls* are endangered by the bite of that old serpent, the devil; and although the wound may appear but slight at the first, yet the venom of sin has entered our system, and unless an antidote be applied, we must inevitably perish eternally. But while such is our deplorable condition by nature, God, in His infinite mercy and love, hath interposed for our salvation. He *so* loved us, that He appointed His only-begotten Son to be the surety and substitute of His people; and when "the fulness of time" was come, the Son of God came down from heaven, not to condemn the world, but that by His obedience, sufferings, and death, He might satisfy divine justicc, and reconcile us to God. And now, like the brazen effigy exhibited in the sight of all Israel, He is revealed in the gospel as lifted up on the cross that all men may believe in Him, and be saved.

Not less significant was the *mode in which the remedy provided for the Israelites was used and applied.* They were commanded to *look* on the brazen serpent; and as many as looked were made whole. In like manner, in order to obtain the spiritual healing which we require, we must *look unto* Jesus Christ, as uplifted on the cross, for the salvation of our perishing souls. The commandment of the gospel to the sinner is, "*Believe* on the Lord Jesus Christ, and thou shalt be saved." It was not the mere lifting up of the serpent which cured the wounded Israelites; they were convinced that they must quickly perish, if they did not *turn their eyes upon* it. Neither is the mere fact, that Christ, while on earth, gave Himself as a sacrifice to atone for our guilt, sufficient to secure the salvation of the sinner. For this purpose, it is essentially necessary that he cordially *believe* that fact, and appropriate to himself the blessings of the Saviour's purchase. Even as the dying Israelites were required to gaze on the brazen serpent, so he must look to, and rest upon the righteousness of Jesus Christ, as all-perfect and all-sufficient. *Thus* depending upon Him, the blood of atonement actually avails to the securing of his pardon and acceptance, and he obtains a title to, and a meetness for the heavenly inheritance. Not that his faith is the meritorious condition of his salvation. No. It is but the means of obtaining it, the hand or instrument with which he receives and holds the imputed righteousness of Christ, for the sake of which alone he is justified in the sight of God.

Looking on the uplifted serpent of brass was the only method appointed by God for the cure of the serpent-stung Israelites. So the *only* way by which sinners can be saved, is by coming to Jesus Christ, and looking to Him as crucified. The disease of sin is incurable by any human or created agency. "Other foundation can no man lay than that is laid, which is Jesus Christ." "Neither is there salvation in any other; for there is none other name under heaven given among men whereby we must be saved."

This method of cure was *free and open* to all the host of Israel. Moses was directed to tell them, that *every one* who looked on the brazen serpent should live. It mattered not how far the disease had gained on him, or how frequently he had been bitten. No sooner did he raise his eyes to the divinely-appointed standard of salvation, than straightway he was healed. Even so is it with respect to the salvation that is in Christ Jesus. It is offered *freely unto all*, without any distinction of character. None are excluded from obtaining an interest in it, save those who by wilful unbelief exclude themselves. The languge of the gospel is, "Look unto Me, and be ye saved, *all the ends of the earth;* for I am God, and there is none else." "Him that cometh unto me, I will in no wise cast out."

This method of cure, *though unlikely to human reason to be successful, was rendered effectual by the power of God.* A serpent of brass could of itself no more heal, than it could wound the Israelites; yet God made their looking on it the means of their escaping death. In like manner, though the connexion between the death of Christ and the pardon of the sinner is not discernible by the eye of reason, yet unto them that are called, is Christ crucified the power of God, and the wisdom of God. The history of Christianity is the history of the achievements of the Cross. And the simple reason is, that the lifted-up sign of redemption is the *divinely-appointed*, and, therefore, the only efficient instrument of conversion and salvation.

Every Israelite who looked to the uplifted serpent in the wilderness *obtained a cure.* Even so, whosoever believeth in the Lord Jesus Christ *shall not perish, but have everlasting life.* He shall be delivered from all the fatal consequences of his natural guilt and pollution ; and though once, like others, "dead in trespasses and sins," yet shall he be quickened by the Holy Spirit, communicated to him from Christ, the living head. Nor over him shall "the second death" have any power. The spiritual life, begun on earth, shall be continued and perfected for ever in heaven. But in vain do we attempt to describe the joy, the glorious effulgence, the magnificence, and bliss of the "salvation which is in Christ Jesus with eternal glory." Here, all language, all conception fails. For "eye hath not seen, nor ear heard, neither have entered into the heart of man, the things which God hath prepared for them that love him."

From what has been advanced, the reader cannot fail to perceive the extreme folly and danger of such as have never looked unto Christ for the salvation that they need. Oh! "how can we escape if we neglect so great salvation?" It is the solemn declaration of our Lord Jesus Christ himself. "He that believeth on him is not condemned; but he that believeth not is condemned already, because he hath not believed in the name of the only-begotten Son of God." How fearful, then, is the doom that hangs over all who seek salvation in ways of their own devising! Infinitely better would it be for such never to have heard of the Mediator, than to stand at last before His dread tribunal, there to be disowned, rejected, and lost. Reader, forget not that a despised salvation will draw down upon you a "far sorer punishment." "Kiss, then, the Son, lest he be angry, and ye perish from the way, when his wrath is kindled but a little." Comply with His merciful invitations, ere His compassions are shut up against you, and His "mercy is clean gone for ever." "Believe on the Lord Jesus

Christ, that you may never perish, but have everlasting life." Let not another sun go down upon your impenitence and unbelief; but resolve *now*, that henceforth you will be the Lord's, and that you will cleave to Him, as your Saviour, your guide, your portion, your all.

While this subject shews the folly and danger of unbelief, it teaches us also that it is the duty of all true Christians *habitually to "look unto Jesus."* So long as they continue in this wilderness world, they are daily receiving fresh wounds from their great Adversary, which, as fiery darts, inflame their inmost souls. But, at all times, an effectual antidote may be obtained, on renewing their application to their heavenly Physician, "whose blood cleanseth from all sin." "Let us," then, "run with patience the race that is set before us, *looking unto Jesus*, the author and finisher of our faith."

"Stretch'd on the cross the Saviour dies,
Hark! His expiring groans arise!
See, from His hands, His feet, His side,
Runs down the sacred crimson tide!

"But life attends the deathful sound,
And flows from every bleeding wound!
The vital stream, how free it flows,
To save and cleanse His rebel foes!

"To suffer in the traitor's place,
To die for man, surprising grace!
Yet pass rebellious angels by—
Oh, why for man, dear Saviour, why?

"And didst Thou bleed, for sinners bleed?
And could the sun behold the deed?
No, he withdrew his sick'ning ray,
And darkness veil'd the mourning day.

"Can I survey this scene of woe,
Where mingling grief and wonder flow:
And yet my heart unmoved remain,
Insensible to love or pain?

"Come, dearest Lord, thy grace impart,
To warm this cold, this stupid heart:
Till all its powers and passions move
In melting grief and ardent love."

STEELE.

"Sweet the moments, rich in blessing,
Which before the cross I spend;
Life, and health, and peace possessing
From the sinner's dying Friend:
Here I'll sit for ever viewing
Mercy's streams in streams of blood;
Precious drops, my soul bedewing,
Plead and claim my peace with God.

"Truly blessed is this station,
Low before His cross to lie;
While I see divine compassion
Floating in His languid eye;
Here it is I find my heaven,
While upon the Lamb I gaze;
Love I much? I've much forgiven,
I'm a miracle of grace!

"Love and grief my heart dividing,
With my tears His feet I'll bathe:
Constant still in faith abiding,
Life deriving from His death.
May I still enjoy this feeling;
In all need to Jesus go;
Prove His wounds each day more healing,
And Himself more deeply know!"

BATTY.

The Paschal Lamb.

1 Cor. v. 7, 8.

"Purge out therefore the old leaven, that ye may be a new lump, as ye are unleavened. For even Christ our passover is sacrificed for us: therefore let us keep the feast, not with old leaven, neither with the leaven of malice and wickedness; but with the unleavened bread of sincerity and truth."

John i. 29.

"The next day John seeth Jesus coming unto him, and saith, Behold the Lamb of God, which taketh away the sin of the world!"

Isa. liii. 7.

"He was oppressed, and he was afflicted; yet he opened not his mouth: he is brought as a lamb to the slaughter, and as a sheep before her shearers is dumb, so he openeth not his mouth."

1 Pet. i. 2.

"Elect according to the foreknowledge of God the Father, through sanctification of the Spirit, unto obedience and sprinkling of the blood of Jesus Christ."

1 Pet. i. 18, 19.

"Forasmuch as ye know that ye were not redeemed with corruptible things, as silver and gold, from your vain conversation received by tradition from your fathers; but with the precious blood of Christ, as of a lamb without blemish and without spot."

Rev. v. 6.

"And I beheld, and, lo, in the midst of the throne and of the four beasts, and in the midst of the elders, stood a Lamb as it had been slain."

Eph. vi. 14, 15.

"Stand therefore, having your loins girt about with truth, and having on the breastplate of righteousness; and your feet shod with the preparation of the gospel of peace."

"Paschal Lamb, by God appointed,
All our sins were on Thee laid!
For the glorious work anointed,
Thou hast full atonement made!

"All Thy people are forgiv'n
Through the virtue of Thy blood;
Open'd is the gate of heaven;
Peace is made 'twixt man and God.

"Jesus, hail, enthroned in glory,
There for ever to abide!
All the heav'nly host adore Thee,
Seated at Thy Father's side.

"There for sinners Thou art pleading,
There Thou dost our place prepare;
Ever for us interceding,
Till in glory we appear."

ANON.

THE PASCHAL LAMB.

OF the three great annual festivals observed by the Jews, that of the Passover was the most ancient and important. It was instituted on their departure from Egypt, in commemoration of their deliverance from the galling servitude in which they had there laboured and groaned for successive centuries, and of the protection granted to their first-born on that night when all the first-born of the Egyptians were destroyed.

The origin, nature, and design of this remarkable ceremony are particularly described in the twelfth chapter of the book of Exodus. The deliverance, which it commemorated was the greatest, and most wonderful, that had ever been vouchsafed to any nation. The Israelites had been reduced to utter subjection; "the Egyptians made them to serve with rigour, and made their lives bitter with hard bondage;" nor, in all human appearance, was there any possibility of escape from "the iron furnace, wherein they were made to serve." The God of Israel, however, resolved to bring them forth with a strong hand, and with an outstretched arm, with signs and wonders, and with mighty works. With this view, He visited their remorseless taskmasters with a series of plagues, following up each successive judgment with a renewed summons to let His people depart out of the land of Egypt.

Nine of these plagues had been successively visited upon them; and yet the heart of Pharaoh was only hardened more and more, and his determination not to let Israel go became more resolute and unbending. But a more fearful infliction was yet to come, which should effectually loosen the iron grasp of the oppressor. For, "at midnight, the Lord smote all the first-born in the land of Egypt, from the first-born of Pharaoh that sat on his throne, unto the first-born of the captive that was in the dungeon; so that Pharaoh rose up in the night, he and all his servants, and all the Egyptians; and there was a great cry in Egypt; for there was not a house where there was not one dead." The Israelites were forewarned, through Moses, that such a visitation was impending; and, in order that they might escape the terrible doom of their oppressors, they were directed to observe a certain protective religious service. It was required that they should take to them every man a lamb, according to the house of their fathers, and after slaying it, to sprinkle its blood upon the lintels and door-posts of their houses: and they were told that the blood would be for a token upon the houses where they were, and the plague would not be upon them to destroy them. Accordingly, wherever the destroying angel recognised this consecrated token, he passed over the house thus marked, without smiting any member of the family it contained. Hence the festival commemorative of this deliverance was called the *Passover*.

But this festival, like the Sabbath and other institutions, had a typical, as well as an historical reference. While reminding the Jews of their great national deliverance, it served, at the same time, to direct their expectations to the great sacrifice for sin by the promised Redeemer. In no previous institution, were the death and atonement of the Son of God so fully developed by typical representation; and never before were those dispositions of mind, with which the sacrifice of the cross must ever be viewed, more clearly pointed out. This is placed beyond all question, by the application which an inspired apostle makes of it, when he says, "Even *Christ, our Passover*, is sacrificed for us." It may be interesting and instructive, therefore, to trace some of the more prominent points of analogy between the paschal sacrifice, and that which it prefigured.

The *victim itself* was to be *a lamb* chosen out of the flock. What could better typify Him, who was raised up from among His brethren, and in whose character the amiable qualities of a lamb shone with such mild and attractive lustre? As a lamb is gentle and without guile, so Jesus "did no violence, neither was there any deceit in His mouth." As a lamb is patient under sufferings, so "when He was reviled, He reviled not again, and when He suffered, He threatened not, but committed Himself to Him that judgeth righteously." Under His severest sufferings, He bowed, without a murmur, beneath the mighty hand of God, while, even in the very crisis of His affliction, nothing was visible but compassion for the guilty; for when He was yet suspended on the cross, instead of accusing His murderers to His Father, He prayed for them, and even pleaded their ignorance in extenuation of their guilt. "Father," He cried, "forgive them, for they know not what they do."

The paschal lamb was required to be "*without blemish.*" In like manner, Christ, who, "through the eternal Spirit, offered Himself unto God," was "without blemish and without spot." He who was "made sin for us," Himself "knew no sin." He who "bare the sins of many," was "holy, harmless, undefiled, and separate from sinners." Though descended from an impure race of ancestors, yet, in consequence of His miraculous conception, He was freed from every taint of original sin. As He advanced in years, the purity of His nature and His life remained unstained, and He died as He lived, a stranger to guilt and to depravity. And it was necessary that "the Lamb of God" should be thus perfect in holiness; otherwise He could never have been a substitute for man, for He would have required an expiation for Himself. But such was the transcendent excellence of His character, that even His bitterest enemies were constrained to confess that there was no fault found in Him, and thereby unwittingly to declare that He was able to perfect for ever all them that are sanctified.

The paschal lamb was appointed to be *slain* on the fourteenth day of the first month, in the evening, in the presence of the whole congregation of Israel. Even so was Christ crucified and slain on the same day as that in which the Jewish passover was celebrated, in the midst, and at the request of "the whole assembly of the congregation of Israel."

The *blood* of the paschal lamb was to be *sprinkled* on the two side-posts, and upper door-posts of the houses, in which it was killed. This was the most essential part of the whole ritual. If the blood was not thus sprinkled, the Israelites were equally exposed to destruction, as though no part of the institution had been complied with. They might have even slain the paschal lamb and feasted on its flesh, but after all, their first-born must have been cut off with those of the Egyptians.

And thus it is, with respect to Jesus Christ our true passover. In order that we may derive any benefit from His atoning sacrifice, it is indispensably necessary to have His *blood applied to our souls.* Even as the blood of the paschal lamb did not save the Israelites by being merely shed in the midst of them, but by being sprinkled by the persons within upon the threshold without, so the shedding of Christ's blood will be of no avail to us unless it be sprinkled on our hearts. Without this, Christ is to us dead in vain; His blood can have no salutary effect with regard to us; and in the judgment of the great day, when "the overflowing scourge shall pass through;" it will be the same to us as though Jesus had never died.

If, however, we be sprinkled with that precious blood, no destruction will ever come near to hurt us. While the angel of God was executing his dread commission in the houses of the Egyptians, and the pride, the hope, the joy of every family was being smitten to death, under the resistless and withering power of an invisible arm, the blood of the paschal lamb, sprinkled on the door-posts, was *the pledge of safety* to the Israelites, and the wrath of God, the pestilence that walketh in darkness, came not nigh them. So shall it be when God shall rise to judgment, when He shall whet His glittering sword, and His hand take hold on vengeance. Then, shall all those be *saved from destruction, who are found sprinkled* with that blood, which speaketh better things than that of Abel. When God seeth this blood upon them, He will pass over all their sins, and will spare them as a man spareth his own son. Though "a thousand shall fall at their side, and ten thousand at their right hand," yet the stroke of offended justice and the bitter pains of eternal death "shall not come nigh unto them. Only with their eyes shall they behold and see the reward of the wicked."

After the paschal lamb had been slain, and its blood sprinkled on the lintels and door-posts of the houses of the Israelites, its flesh was to be *used as food*. So by faith does the believer feed upon Jesus Christ, and obtain an interest in all the blessed effects of His atoning sacrifice. "Except ye *eat* the flesh of the Son of man and drink his blood, ye have no life in you. Whoso eateth my flesh and drinketh my blood hath eternal life: and I will raise him up at the last day."

The paschal lamb was to be prepared as food by *roasting it with fire.* What could better prefigure the *flames of the Divine wrath,* which raged so hotly against the immaculate Lamb of God, when, as the victim of a world's transgressions, He endured those agonising *sufferings,* which wrung out from Him that most mournful and piteous cry that ever asçended to heaven from earth, "My God, my God, why hast thou forsaken me?"

It was required that "*not a bone of the paschal lamb should be broken.*" So, in the account of our Lord's crucifixion, the evangelist informs us, that, "when the soldiers came to Jesus and saw that he was dead already, they brake not his legs;" and thus, it is added, was fulfilled that which had been written, "*A bone of him shall not be broken.*" This circumstance, though minute in itself, serves to demonstrate, that in the death of Christ there was an exact fulfilment of the passover institution.

The paschal lamb was to be *eaten with unleavened bread, and bitter herbs.* The immediate design of this part of the ritual was, doubtless, to remind the Israelites of their grievous bondage in Egypt, and their haste in leaving it, which allowed them no time to prepare their bread by a process of fermentation. But, besides this, it was fitted to convey a perpetual intimation of those dispositions with which the spiritual Israel ought ever to feast upon the True Passover, even with the *unleavened bread of sincerity and truth*, with *contrition* and *godly sorrow for sin*, and with a sacred resolve to mortify their corrupt desires, to deny themselves, to take up the cross, and to bear it with patience and cheerfulness amid all the trials and hardships of their desert pilgrimage.

The paschal lamb was to be eaten by the Israelites *in a standing posture*—with their *loins girded*, their *shoes on their feet, and their staff in their hand*—in token of their readiness to depart from Egypt, and begin their pilgrimage through the desert to the Land of Promise. Even thus is it with all who have obtained deliverance from an infinitely worse than Egyptian bondage—from the tyranny of Satan, the slavery of sin, and the dread of eternal death. They are separated from the world, that they may commence their heavenly pilgrimage, under the guidance of the Captain of their salvation, who, in the hour of His grace, summons them to arise and depart. *Girding up the loins of their minds*, and having their *feet shod with the preparation of the gospel of peace*, they are to *take up the pilgrim's staff*, and go forth, as men travelling through strange and hostile regions, to a distant home. Nor will their course terminate till the hour of death, when the scenes of time shall fade away from their view, and immortality shall unfold to them its visions of splendour and of joy.

Numerous other points of similitude might be indicated between the typical and the true Passover; but those we have condescended upon clearly shew that this religious observance was a true mirror of the mystery of redemption, exhibiting the Son of God as the great sacrificial victim of a world's transgressions. "It was, in fact," as it has been justly said, an "annual prophecy, addressed not to the ear but to the eye, of His life, passion, and death."

And now that that prophecy has passed into the clear light of an actual history, it becomes us seriously to inquire, whether our souls have been sprinkled with the peace-speaking and life-giving blood of Him, in whom it has been so strikingly fulfilled. For, "if he who despised Moses' law died without mercy, under two or three witnesses; of how much sorer punishment, suppose ye, shall he be thought worthy, who hath trodden under foot the Son of God, and hath counted the blood of the covenant, wherewith he was sanctified, an unholy thing, and done despite to the Spirit of grace?" For those who neglect so great salvation, "there remaineth no more sacrifice for sin, but a certain fearful looking for of judgment, and fiery indignation, to devour the adversaries of God." Without a moment's delay, therefore, let us lay hold on "the blood of sprinkling;" for when the midnight cry of Egypt is heard, it will then be too late. "*Now* is the accepted time: *now* is the day of salvation."

"Not all the blood of beasts
  On Jewish altars slain,
Could give the guilty conscience peace,
  Or wash away the stain.

"But Christ the heav'nly Lamb,
Takes all our sins away:
A sacrifice of nobler name,
And richer blood than they.

"Believing, we rejoice
To see the curse remove:
We bless the Lamb with cheerful voice,
And sing His dying love."

WATTS.

"Now our paschal Lamb is He,
And by Him alone we live,
Who to death upon the tree,
For our sake Himself did give.
Faith His blood strikes on our door,
Death dares never harm us more.

"To the supper of the Lord,
Gladly will we come to-day,
The word of peace is now restored,
The old leaven is put away:
Christ will be our food alone,
Faith no life but His doth own."

LUTHER, 1524.

"Lo, the destroying angel flies
To Pharaoh's stubborn land:
The pride and flow'r of Egypt dies
By his avenging hand.

"He pass'd the tents of Jacob o'er,
Nor pour'd the wrath divine:
He saw the blood on every door,
And bless'd the peaceful sign.

Thus the appointed Lamb must bleed
  To break the Egyptian yoke:
Thus Israel is from bondage freed
  And 'scapes the angel's stroke.

"Lord, since my heart is sprinkled too,
  With blood so rich as Thine,
Justice no longer will pursue
  This guilty soul of mine.

"Jesus our passover was slain,
  And has at once procured
Freedom from Satan's heavy chains,
  And God's avenging sword."

WATTS.

The Goël, or Kinsman Redeemer.

HEB. ii. 14, 15.

"Forasmuch then as the children are partakers of flesh and blood, he also himself likewise took part of the same; that through death he might destroy him that had the power of death, that is, the devil; and deliver them who, through fear of death, were all their lifetime subject to bondage."

JOB xix. 25.

"For I know that my Redeemer liveth, and that he shall stand at the latter day upon the earth."

LUKE i. 68–71.

"Blessed be the Lord God of Israel; for he hath visited and redeemed his people, and hath raised up an horn of salvation for us in the house of his servant David; as he spake by the mouth of his holy prophets which have been since the world began; that we should be saved from our enemies, and from the hand of all that hate us."

1 PET. i. 3–5.

"Blessed be the God and Father of our Lord Jesus Christ, which, according to his abundant mercy, hath begotten us again unto a lively hope, by the resurrection of Jesus Christ from the dead, to an inheritance incorruptible, and undefiled, and that fadeth not away, reserved in heaven for you, who are kept by the power of God through faith unto salvation, ready to be revealed in the last time."

REV. v. 9, 10.

"And they sung a new song, saying, Thou art worthy to take the book, and to open the seals thereof; for thou wast slain, and hast redeemed us to God by thy blood out of every kindred, and tongue, and people and nation; and hast made us unto our God, kings and priests: and we shall reign on the earth."

"Enslaved by sin and bound in chains,
  Beneath its dreadful tyrant sway,
And doom'd to everlasting pains
  We wretched guilty captives lay.

"Nor gold nor gems could buy our peace;
  Nor the whole world's collected store
Suffice to purchase our release;
  A thousand worlds were all too poor.

"Jesus, the Lord, the mighty God,
  An all-sufficient ransom paid:
Invalu'd price! His precious blood
  For vile rebellious traitors shed.

"Jesus the sacrifice became,
  To rescue guilty souls from hell;
The spotless, bleeding, dying Lamb,
  Beneath avenging justice fell.

"Amazing goodness! Love divine!
  O may our grateful hearts adore
The matchless grace, nor yield to sin,
  Nor wear its cruel fetters more!

"Dear Saviour, let Thy love pursue
  The glorious work it has begun,
Each secret lurking foe subdue,
  And let our hearts be Thine alone."

STEELE.

THE GOËL, OR KINSMAN REDEEMER.

UNDER the Jewish polity it was provided, that when an Israelite was, from poverty, or any other circumstance, unable to act for himself, or to assert his own rights, his nearest kinsman should bear the responsibilities of his redemption. The person who did so was denominated his *goël*, or *kinsman redeemer;* and in this legal relationship, a variety of very peculiar rights and responsibilities devolved upon him. For example, he was enjoined to ransom the inheritance of his impoverished relative when it happened to be forfeited or mortgaged, to redeem his person when in a state of servitude, to marry his widow and raise up seed to him when he died without children, and to avenge his blood when slain by an enemy. In all these things, the goël stood in the place of his relative, and acted as his legal representative.

But this provision of the Mosaic law was designed to be a very clear and beautiful type of the office of our glorious Mediator. Nor is it without reason that this very name goël is so frequently applied to Him in those passages of the Hebrew scriptures, which speak of Him as our Redeemer. By assuming the nature of man, He became "flesh of our flesh, and bone of our bone." "As the children were partakers of flesh and blood, he also himself likewise took part of the same." Having, in the fulness of time, thus taken our nature into a personal and indissoluble union with that which belonged to Him as God, He became our blood-relation, our Kinsman after the flesh, and as such, the rights and duties connected with our redemption devolved upon Him. Hence it became Him to fulfil all righteousness, as our Surety and Representative; and now, in virtue of the infinitely valuable ransom which He paid to Divine justice on our behalf, "with him is plenteous redemption, and he shall redeem Israel from all his iniquities." But let us inquire more particularly how Christ, as our goël, has accomplished our redemption, and still fulfils to us the duties of a kinsman.

It belonged to the goël under the law to redeem the mortgaged inheritance of his impoverished relative ; and, in like maner, it behoved Christ *to restore our forfeited inheritance of eternal life.* Man, as he came forth from the hand of his Creator, was rich in the birthright which gave him an eternity of blessedness for his possession. But "the gold has become dim, the most fine gold is changed." Having sold away his birthright for one morsel of forbidden fruit, his fair inheritance is alienated, and not one farthing can he advance towards buying it back again. Not even angels could deliver us from that spiritual destitution and wretchedness, into which we had so recklessly plunged ourselves. But, what neither angels nor men could accomplish, the Son of God, as our goël, has completely effected. "He restored that which he took not away." All that our impoverished nature had lost by reason of Adam's fall, He has redeemed with His own inestimably precious blood.

> "The ransom was paid down : the fund of heaven,
> Heaven's inexhaustible, exhausted fund,
> Amazing, and amazed, pour'd forth the price ;
> All price beyond !"

Nay, such is the grace of our Divine Redeemer, that He has not simply restored our lost inheritance, but vastly improved it. He hath raised us to a happiness, more exquisite and exalted, than Adam enjoyed in his original state of innocence; for, instead of paradise, He has purchased for us heaven. He has brought life and immortality to light by His gospel, and secured to us an inheritance lovelier and more glorious far than even Eden in all its primeval beauty—"an inheritance incorruptible, undefiled, and that fadeth not away, reserved in heaven for them, who are kept by the power of God, through faith unto salvation."

While Christ has thus redeemed for us our forfeited inheritance, so has He, like the goël under the law, *redeemed us from the slavery of sin.* Men are by nature in a state of spiritual bondage; sin reigns in their mortal bodies, and they yield their members servants to uncleanness and to iniquity. Having been led captive by their great spiritual Adversary, they are, as it were, shut up in prison, and bound by the fetters of sin, which no created power can break, no created ingenuity unlock.

"Chains are the portion of revolted man—
Stripes and a dungeon."

But from this inglorious servitude, our Kinsman in His love, and in His pity, redeemed us, when He became a bond-servant in our room, and "gave Himself a ransom for all." Had He merely secured our title to the heavenly inheritance, His work would manifestly have been imperfect; for He could not put us in possession of it, and restore us to happiness, without first striking off our fetters, and opening our prison doors. It behoved Him, therefore, not only to redeem the inheritance to us, but us to the inheritance. Accordingly, we are assured, that it is His office to set us free, and that "if the Son make us free, we shall be free indeed." "The Spirit of the Lord is upon him, because the Lord hath anointed him, to proclaim liberty to the captives, and the opening of the prison to them that are bound." While His atoning sacrifice opened up a new and living way into the kingdom of heaven, it also purchased the gift of the Holy Ghost, whose sanctifying influence on our hearts can alone make us "meet to be partakers of the inheritance of the saints in light." "We are sanctified through the offering up of the body of Christ." "He gave himself for us, that he might redeem us from all iniquity, and purify us unto himself a peculiar people, zealous of good works." By the almighty influence of His grace in them that believe on His name, He breaks off the fetters of sin, throws open the prison doors, and bids them come forth, and walk to and fro, in the "glorious liberty of the children of God."

But it behoved Christ, as our Goël, not only to redeem our forfeited inheritance to us, and us to the inheritance, but also *to render us fruitful in every good work.* If an Israelite died without children, the law expressly enjoined the Goël to marry his widow, and raise up seed unto him, that his name might not perish. In allusion to this, Jehovah is represented as saying unto His ancient people,—"Now, when I passed by thee, and looked upon thee, behold, thy time was the time of love; and I spread my skirt over thee: yea, I sware unto thee, and entered into a covenant with thee, and thou becamest mine." Previously to the violation of the first covenant, our nature was fruitful unto

God; but now, alas! the heart of man is barren as the flinty rock. The Most High looked upon the earth, and behold it was corrupt, for all flesh had corrupted his way upon the earth. It may be truly said of all men in their unregenerate state, "They conceive mischief, and bring forth vanity." So long as they are "in the flesh, the motions of sins, which are by the law, work in their members to bring forth fruit unto death." But, from this alarming state of sterility and barrenness, our kinsman Redeemer voluntarily and cheerfully consented to deliver us by uniting us to Himself. This indeed was a most unequal alliance, and numerous and most formidable difficulties had to be encountered ere it could be consolidated; but, since it was requisite for the purposes of redemption, He manifested His unparalleled love to us, by completely removing every obstacle out of the way. And now, in consequence of their union to Him, all who believe are "become dead to the law by the body of Christ, that they should be married to another, even to him who is raised from the dead, that they should bring forth fruit unto God." "He that abideth in me," He says, "and I in him, the same bringeth forth much fruit; for, without me, ye can do nothing." Now, "our Maker is our husband; the Lord of hosts is his name: and our Redeemer the Holy One of Israel: the God of the whole earth shall he be called." He hath betrothed us unto Himself for ever; and, therefore, she that was "barren hath born seven," and many "are the children of the desolate."

But Christ has still further fulfilled the duties of a kinsman Redeemer to us, *by avenging our blood on our murderer Satan.* According to the Mosaic law, the nearest kinsman of any one who happened to be slain was required to pursue the manslayer, and if he overtook him, to avenge the wrong by putting him to death. Need we here remind the reader that in this, as well as in the other duties that devolved on the near kinsman, we discover a striking representation of the office of Christ? Although created immortal, the whole human race was slain by Satan, when, through his subtlety, he beguiled our first parents into that first act of disobedience against the great Creator, which "brought death into the world and all our woe." It seems to be with reference to this slaughter of mankind, that Christ said of the devil, "He was a murderer from the beginning." As it was through him that man was first seduced into sin, which is the cause of death, so on that account our great Adversary is said to "have the power of death." But, by "putting away sin," our kinsman Redeemer has removed at the same time all its direful consequences "Through death he hath destroyed him that had the power of death, that is, the devil, and delivered them, who through fear of death, were all their lifetime subject to bondage." "And he saw that there was no man, and wondered that there was no intercessor; therefore his arm brought salvation unto him, and his righteousness it sustained him. For he put on righteousness as a breastplate, and an helmet of salvation upon his head; and he put on the garments of vengeance for clothing, and was clad with zeal as a cloak." This glorious Avenger of our blood has not only pursued, overtaken, and gained the mastery over the great manslayer, but restored life to the slain, and through the merit of His atonement and the power of His Spirit, He enables even the most feeble and timid of them to become more than conquerors over the wicked one. "The sting of death is sin, and the strength of sin is the law; but thanks be to God who giveth us the victory, through our Lord Jesus Christ."

Thus it appears that what the earthly Goël was required by the Mosaic law to do for his impoverished relative, our heavenly Goël, our all-gracious Redeemer has done, and is, in some sense, still doing for His poor kindred. He has redeemed their inheritance to them, and them to their inheritance; He has rendered them fruitful in every good work, and avenged their blood on their great adversary, who is the murderer of souls.

And who can contemplate the amazing condescension and love of the Son of God in thus becoming our Kinsman, and espousing our cause, without the liveliest emotions? Should not our faith, as it gazes on our great Deliverer, lift aloud its voice in accents of everlasting praise? And how earnestly solicitous should we be to walk worthy of the exalted privileges which He hath so dearly purchased, and so freely bestowed upon us! When we consider that we are not our own, but bought with a price, even the precious blood of Christ, as of a lamb without blemish and without spot, oh! what manner of persons ought we to be in all holy conversation and godliness? Let us therefore glorify God in our bodies and in our spirits which are His. Let our citzenship be in heaven: and "reckoning ourselves to be dead indeed unto sin, but alive unto God through Jesus Christ our Lord, let not sin reign in our mortal bodies, that we should obey it in the lusts thereof;" but let us walk as the redeemed of the Lord, "as free, and not using our liberty for a cloak of maliciousness, but as the servants of God."

If we have not yet been redeemed from the curse of the law, but are still sunk in sin, and shackled with its deadly weight, it is, most assuredly, not from any want of efficacy in the blood of the cross, or from any defect of love or power in our glorious Deliverer, but simply because we are unwilling to avail ourselves of the emancipation, which He died to purchase, and now lives to bestow. Let us, therefore, no longer continue in our present degrading servitude, lest He, whom we have chosen as our master, should hereafter bind us hand and foot, and cast us into the prison of hell, whose adamantine gates shall never be opened, and to the inhabitants of which the gladsome sound, "Go forth," will never come. This very day, this very hour, let us choose whom we will serve. Is there any room for hesitation here? Slavery and freedom—life and death—heaven and hell—these are the alternatives we have before us. Let us choose that which is good. The time for deliberation will swiftly pass, and our choice become irrevocable.

"Plunged in a gulf of dark despair
We wretched sinners lay,
Without one cheerful gleam of hope,
Or spark of glimm ring day.

"With pitying eyes, the Prince of Grace
Beheld our helpless grief;
He saw, and (O amazing love!)
He ran to our relief.

"Down from the shining seats above
With joyful haste He fled,
Enter'd the grave in mortal flesh,
And dwelt among the dead.

"Oh! for this love let rocks and hills
Their lasting silence break,
And all harmonious human tongues
The Saviour's praises speak.

"Angels, assist our mighty joys,
Strike all your harps of gold;
But when you raise your highest notes
His love can ne'er be told."

WATTS.

"Thou strong and loving Son of Man,
Redeemer from the bonds of sin,
'Tis Thou the living spark dost fan
That sets my heart on fire within.
Thou openest heaven once more to men,
The soul's true home, Thy kingdom, Lord,
And I can trust and hope again,
And feel myself akin to God."

AFTER NOVALIS—1795.

"Then shall the day-spring rise, before whose beams
The darkness of the world is past; for, hark!
Seraphs and angel-choirs with symphonies
Acclaiming of ten thousand golden harps
Amid the bursting clouds of heaven reveal'd,
At once in glory jubilant,—they sing:
'God the Redeemer liveth! He who took
Man's nature on Him, and in human shroud
Veil'd His immortal glory! He is risen—
God the Redeemer liveth! And behold
The gates of life and immortality
Opened to all that breathe.'"

W. L. BOWLES.

"Now begin the heav'nly theme;
Sing aloud the Saviour's name,
Ye who Jesus' kindness prove,
Sing of His Redeeming Love.

"Ye who see the Father's grace
Beaming in the Saviour's face,
As to Canaan on ye move,
Praise and bless Redeeming Love.

"Ye who long, alas! have been
Willing slaves of death and sin,
See the guilt and curse remove,
Cancell'd by Redeeming Love.

"Mourning souls, refrain your tears;
Trembling hearts, dismiss your fears;
Now from bliss no longer rove;
Listen to Redeeming Love.

"Hither, then, your tribute bring;
Strike aloud each joyful string;
Saints below and saints above,
Join to praise Redeeming Love.

"When His Spirit leads us home,
When we to His glory come,
He shall all the fulness prove
Of our Lord's Redeeming Love."

LANGFORD.

The City of Refuge.

DEUT. xxxiii. 27.

"The eternal God is thy refuge, and underneath are the everlasting arms; and he shall thrust out the enemy from before thee: and shall say, Destroy them."

HEB. vi. 18.

"That by two immutable things, in which it was impossible for God to lie, we might have a strong consolation, who have fled for refuge to lay hold upon the hope set before us."

JOHN xv. 4.

"Abide in me."

ZECHARIAH ix. 12.

"Turn you to the strong-hold, ye prisoners of hope."

"How oft have sin and Satan strove
To rend my soul from Thee, my God
But everlasting is Thy love,
And Jesus seals it with His blood.

"The oath and promise of the Lord
Join to confirm the wondrous grace;
Eternal pow'r performs the word,
And fills all heav'n with endless praise.

"Amidst temptations sharp and long,
My soul to this dear refuge flies;
Hope is my anchor firm and strong,
While tempests blow and billows rise.

"The gospel bears my spirits up;
A faithful and unchanging God
Lays the foundation for my hope
In oaths, and promises, and blood."

WATTS.

THE CITY OF REFUGE.

IN the earlier stages of the national economy of the Jews, the execution of the original enactment, that "whoso sheddeth man's blood, by man shall his blood be shed," devolved on the nearest male relative of the person whose life had been taken away. If he did not avenge the wrong by putting the guilty person to death, he was considered infamous. Hence he bore the Hebrew appellation *Goël*, which signifies *spotted* or *contaminated*, until he slew the manslayer, and thus satisfied the requirements of the law, which demanded life for life.

In order, however, to prevent the effects of rash resentment, and to provide for the protection of the unfortunate manslayer, who, without malice or design, had been instrumental in taking away the life of his neighbour, it pleased God in course of time to set apart six cities of refuge, three on either side of Jordan, to which the manslayer might flee as his sanctuary from the avenger. These cities belonged to the tribe of Levi, and were intended not for the Israelites alone, but for the heathen " stranger, and for the sojourner in the land, that every one," whosoever he might be, " that killed any person unawares, might flee thither." They were so situated, that, from the remotest corner of the land, the manslayer might reach one of them in a few hours. That nothing might retard his flight, great care was taken to keep the roads, by which they were approached, open and good. The Jewish Rabbis inform us, that, in those places where there happened to be water, bridges were erected; and that at every cross-road, posts were set up with the words, " Refuge," " Refuge," inscribed on them, so that there might be no doubt as to the right direction in which to flee. Once entered within the gates of the city, the hand of individual violence was arrested, and punishment, could only be inflicted by the decision of the judges, whose duty it was to examine and determine all such cases. If, upon trial, the person were found guilty of wilful and premeditated violence, he was at once delivered up to the avenger of blood. If, on the other hand, it appeared that he, who fled to the city of refuge, had slain his neighbour "unwittingly," he was to remain in the city, till the death of the officiating high priest, and then to "return into the land of his possession." If, however, he ventured beyond its precincts before that period, his protection was forfeited, and the long-suspended sword of the avenger might again be unsheathed with impunity against him.

We have no design whatever to enter into the question whether these cities of refuge were, strictly speaking, intended to be typical of the arrangements and provisions of Divine mercy for the spiritual wants of mankind in the work of the Lord Jesus Christ. We refer to them simply for the purpose of illustration, and, in doing so, we shall only be following the example of the writer of the epistle to the Hebrews, who, in figuratively describing the character of true believers, says, "They have *fled for refuge* to lay hold upon the hope set before them,"—words which obviously contain a very beautiful allusion to the cities in question. In what remains of this chapter, therefore, our object will be to state and illustrate a few of the analogies or resemblances, which may be traced between the city of rcfuge, under the Jewish polity, and Jesus Christ, to whom the awakened sinner under the gospel, flees, as the hope set before him.

The city of refuge was provided for those who were *in circumstances of imminent danger.* No sooner did the manslayer take away the life of his neighbour, than he placed his own at the mercy of the avenger of blood; and, until the city of refuge received him within its walls, his jeopardy was extreme. For, at any moment, the avenger might overtake him, and plunge his sword into his bosom. Even so is it with the sinner. By violating the precepts of the Divine law, he has rendered himself obnoxious to the inexorable justice of an angry God, whose wrath it is alike impossible for him to escape or to endure. For, the decree of Heaven against all the workers of iniquity is, "The soul that sinneth, it shall die." "Cursed is every one that continueth not in all things which are written in the book of the law to do them." This condemnatory sentence every individual of the human race has incurred, and the justice of God cries aloud for vengeance. The transgressor is every moment of his existence at the mercy of the spoiler. Death, the avenger of the law, is in hot pursuit; and should he be overtaken before obtaining an interest by faith in the imputed righteousness of Immanuel, he is for ever undone.

Mankind, however, are naturally insensible to the appalling danger which thus hangs over them. Multitudes, who readily enough admit that they are sinners, seem to imagine that no danger is to be apprehended, and soothe themselves with the vague expectation, that since God is merciful, they will in the end be enabled to reach some place of safety or some path of escape. But amid all their fancied security, they are "dead in trespasses and sins," and "the wrath of God abideth upon them." Their danger is most terrible and urgent, how unconscious of it soever they may be. Like a sleeper on the brink of a fearful precipice, they are indulging in vain dreams of security, though all the while destruction, dark, stern, and irremediable, is threatening to swallow them up.

But no sooner does an individual become sensible of his real condition, as a condemned and hell-deserving sinner, than there is an end to this false and perilous security, and, like the manslayer in Judea, pursued by the avenger of blood, he pauses not for a single instant, till he obtains an entrance into the appointed City of Refuge, even Jesus Christ, in whom alone he can be secure from the avenging wrath of Almighty God. Fixing his view steadfastly on this glorious object, he calls into redoubled action the energies of his spiritual nature, and with all the earnestness of one whose eternal interests are at stake, he speeds perseveringly his heavenward course. He "counts all things but loss, that he may win Christ, and be found in him;" and his language is, "O Lord thou art my refuge and my portion in the land of the living. Attend unto my cry; for I am brought very low; deliver me from my persecutors; for they are stronger than I."

As the city of refuge, under the Jewish polity, was provided for those who were in circumstances of imminent danger, so the *most ample directions and facilities were afforded for reaching it.* The cities of refuge were scattered through the territories of Israel at convenient distances, so that one or other of them "lay within half a day's journey of every part of the land." The roads which led to them were made of unusual width, and kept in repair by the public authorities, so that no obstacle might impede the progress of him who was escaping for his life. But if, perchance, a passing doubt might harass him, there met his view, at every turn, some friendly pillar, bearing the inscription, "Refuge!" "Refuge!" and pointing his wandering eye or weary step toward the object of his anxious search. Besides, as we have already remarked, we are told that all were allowed to avail themselves of the privilege of fleeing to these cities, that they were designed for the stranger and the sojourner, as well as for the Israelites themselves, and that when an individual, who had been the innocent cause of his neighbour's death, repaired to one of them, and made known his case to the elders who resided in it, he was at once admitted.

In all these arrangements for the escape of the manslayer, we are presented with a beautiful representation of the facilities, which are given us, in fleeing to that refuge which God, in His infinite mercy, has appointed for sinners ready to perish. Jesus is a refuge near at hand, "not far from every one of us." In order to find Him, no toilsome pilgrimage requires to be performed, nor need any of us say in our heart, "Who shall ascend into heaven? (that is, to bring Christ down from above,) or who shall descend into the deep? (that is, to bring up Christ again from the dead.)" "Behold," saith He Himself, by the prophet, "I bring near my righteousness, and my salvation shall not tarry." The way to Him is open—a new and living way—a highway which the Lord hath commanded to be made; and on it no stone of stumbling is to be found, which can in any degree impede the sinner's flight to the blessed shelter of the cross. "Every valley is exalted, and every mountain and hill made low; and the crooked is made straight, and the rough places plain."

Not only have all obstructions been removed out of the way, but the clearest and most explicit directions are given for our guidance. Jehovah Himself, the fountain of all wisdom, discovers to us "the path of life," and "leads us in the way everlasting."

His word is "a light unto our feet, and a lamp unto our path;" it is a *way-mark*, pointing, with unerring finger, to the Divinely-appointed Refuge for the endangered soul.

And the task prescribed to us is as simple as the direction is clear. Such is the ineffable value of the salvation that is in Christ Jesus, that it would not have been surprising though the bestowal of it had been fettered with conditions the most complicated; but such is the grace of our Lord Jesus Christ, that the way of acceptance and escape is reduced to one simple act—that of believing the testimony which God has given concerning Him. "Believe," it is said, "in the Lord Jesus Christ, and thou shalt be saved." "God so loved the world, that he gave his only-begotten Son, that whosoever believeth in him might not perish, but have everlasting life." How divinely simple is the mode appointed by infinite wisdom for our obtaining a participation in the blessings of the great Salvation!

"Oh! how unlike the complex works of man,
Heaven's easy, artless, unencumber'd plan!
No meretricious graces to beguile,
No clustering ornaments to clog the pile,

From ostentation as from weakness free,
It stands like the cerulean arch we see—
Majestic in its own simplicity.
Inscrib'd above the portal from afar,
Conspicuous as the brightness of a star,
Legible only by the light they give,
Stand the soul-quickening words—BELIEVE AND LIVE!"

COWPER.

As the mode of obtaining an interest in Christ is amazingly simple, so the invitations to flee to Him are unrestrictedly free. In Him is salvation for those that are afar off, as well as for them that are nigh. He stands, as it were, with outstretched arms, in the midst of the earth, that sinners everywhere may know that He is not beyond their reach. His language is, "Him that cometh unto me I will in nowise cast out." "Come unto me, all ye that labour and are heavy laden, and I will give you rest." "Look unto me, and be ye saved, all the ends of the earth." Not one is excluded; no, not even the chief of sinners. The invitations to accept of His salvation are wide as the earth, impartial and free as the bounty of our Father in heaven, who "maketh his sun to rise on the evil and on the good, and sendeth rain on the just and on the unjust." If men perish at last, they perish through their own fault.

Another striking resemblance between Christ and the city of refuge may be traced in *the completeness and certainty of the protection provided.* The moment that the wretched manslayer passed the gate of the refuge city, he was safe from the stroke of the avenger. But an hour before, his throbbing heart beat high with the impulse of fear; now, however, he might stand secure and unmoved within the peaceful habitation. His life was henceforth sacred, and any attempt upon it would have involved the most aggravated contempt of the great Lawgiver of Israel. Within the city, everything necessary was provided for his sustenance; and no weapons were allowed to be made or sold therein. Everything, in short, was done to make it at once a safe and an agreeable asylum to him who happened to "smite his neighbour unwittingly, and hated him not before-time." No other place, however, could afford him a legal shelter from the rage of his pursuer.

And equally secure is the condition of those who, for their immortal welfare, flee, in faith and penitence, to Jesus Christ as their Refuge and Redeemer. Having once found rest in Him, they are as free from danger as though they had never sinned. Divine justice, which, like the avenger of blood, had been pursuing them, no longer fills them with dismay, its demands having been fully satisfied, when, in the room of sinners, the Son of God freely and voluntarily paid

"The rigid satisfaction—death for death."

Nor has the Divine law any power to alarm them. From its awful curse, also, Jesus has redeemed them, He himself "being first made a curse for them." And even now, as its thunders roll around them, they are enabled, in humble reliance on His infinite merit, to exclaim, with a joyful, though trembling confidence, "O thou enemy, destructions are come to a perpetual end." "Who shall lay anything to the charge of God's elect? It is God that justifieth. Who is he that condemneth? It is Christ that died, yea, rather, that is risen again, who is even at the right hand of God, who also maketh intercession for us. Who shall separate us from the love of Christ? Shall tribulation, or distress, or persecution, or famine, or nakedness, or peril, or sword? Nay, in all these things we are more than conquerors, through him that loved us. For we are persuaded that neither death, nor life, nor angels, nor principalities, nor powers, nor things present, nor things to come, nor height, nor depth, nor any other creature, shall be able to separate us from the love of God, which is in Christ Jesus our Lord."

Christ is a city of refuge, whence, if a man once enter it, he shall go no more out. "I give unto my sheep," He declares, "eternal life, and they shall never perish, neither shall any man pluck them out of my hand; my Father, which gave them me, is greater than all, and no man is able to pluck them out of my Father's hand. I and my Father are one." In Christ there is abundant provision made for every want; for "God will supply all our need according to his own riches in glory by Christ Jesus." At the same time, however, it behoves us to remember, that it is they only who are in Him—united to Him by a true and holy faith—who are shielded from the sword of God's avenging justice. "Neither is there salvation in any other, for there is none other name given under heaven among men, whereby they must be saved." "He that believeth not the Son shall not see life, but the wrath of God abideth on him."

Such are a few of those analogies, or resemblances, which obtain between our New Testament Refuge, and the cities of sanctuary under the law. There are some important points, however, in which the former far excels the latter. The Jewish cities of refuge were appointed for the benefit of those only who had committed homicide by accident, and without malice or design. If, upon examination by the appointed judges, any person who had fled to one of them were found guilty of murder, nothing could save him from the stroke of the avenger; even the altar itself, in such a case, afforded no refuge, and no commutation whatever was admissible. But observe how, in this respect, Jesus has the pre-eminence. He is an asylum for sinners of every class and description. It matters not how numerous and aggravated soever their iniquities may have been. Only let them, by true faith and repentance, seek to Him, and they shall at once be admitted to a participation in the fulness of those blessings which He has to bestow. In this city of sanctuary, Manasseh, who made Jerusalem run down with blood, Mary Magdalene, the malefactor on the cross, and many others, who had been guilty of the vilest and most atrocious crimes, have obtained refuge, and been for ever delivered from the wrath and curse of the Almighty.

The manslayer might be overtaken in his flight to the city of refuge, and be slain by the avenger of blood. But the sinner has only to direct the eye of faith to Christ, and from that moment he is as safe from wrath as though he were in heaven itself. The Jewish city of refuge defended only the natural life of the manslayer, which, in a few years at most, would at all events, be restored to Him who gave it. But all who flee for refuge to Christ are delivered from the eternal death of the soul, and made partakers of a life that shall never, never come to an end. Subsequently to the death of the high-priest the manslayer was to "return, and come unto his own city, and unto his own house, unto the city from which he fled." But our High Priest is one that never dies; and all the blessings of His great salvation are freely and for ever given.

Reader, the illustration which we have thus given of Jesus Christ, as our City of Refuge, presents the strongest possible motives to all to come without delay, and lay hold of His great salvation. What tongue can express the magnitude of the danger that impends over you, so long as you are not found in Him. The destroying angel pursues you with rapid step: the avenger of sin is at hand; his voice is heard declaring, "vengeance is mine, I will repay:" and, if the mercy of Heaven prevent not, he will seize you as his lawful prey, bind you hand and foot, and carry you down to the dark and dismal mansions of despair, where you shall feel, to your sad experience, that "it is," indeed, "a fearful thing to fall into the hands of the living God." "Escape," then, sinner, "for thy life: look not behind thee, neither stay thou in all the plain:" flee with speed to the city of refuge, which God has prepared for you. It is "a city fortified," and it is "nigh at hand." Its gates stand open continually for the reception of every sinner in whose heart there is a sincere and earnest desire for refuge: and on their lofty arches are inscribed the inviting words, "Turn ye to the strong-hold, ye prisoners of hope: even to-day do I declare that I will render double unto thee."

"A sure strong-hold our God is He,
A trusty shield and weapon;
Our help He'll be and set us free
From every ill can happen.
That old malicious foe
Intends us deadly woe;
Arm'd with the strength of hell
And deepest craft as well,
On earth is not his fellow.

"Through our own force we nothing can,
Straight were we lost for ever;
But for us fights the proper Man
By God sent to deliver.
Ask ye who this may be?
Christ Jesus named is He,
Of Sabaoth the Lord;
Sole God to be adored;
'Tis He must win the battle.'

"And were the world with devils fill'd
All eager to devour us,
Our souls to fear should little yield,
They cannot overpower us.
Their dreaded prince no more
Can harm us as of yore;
Look grim as e'er he may,
Doom'd is his ancient sway;
A word can overthrow him.

"Still shall they leave that Word His might,
  And yet no thanks shall merit;
Still is He with us in the fight,
  By His good gifts and Spirit.
E'en should they take our life,
Goods, honour, children, wife—
Though all of these be gone,
Yet nothing have they won,
  God's kingdom ours abideth!

LUTHER.

Translated by Catherine Winkworth.

The Good Shepherd.

PS. xxiii. 1.

"The Lord is my shepherd: I shall not want."

ISA. xl. 11.

"He shall feed his flock like a shepherd; he shall gather the lambs with his arm, and carry them in his bosom, and shall gently lead those that are with young."

EZEK. xxxiv. 22.

"Therefore will I save my flock, and they shall be no more a prey."

ZECH. xiii. 7.

"Awake, O sword, against my Shepherd, and against the man that is my fellow, saith the Lord of hosts: smite the shepherd, and the sheep shall be scattered, and I will turn mine hand upon the little ones."

JOHN x. 11–16.

"I am the good Shepherd: the good Shepherd giveth his life for the sheep. But he that is an hireling, and not the shepherd, whose own the sheep are not, seeth the wolf coming, and leaveth the sheep and fleeth; and the wolf catcheth them, and scattereth the sheep. The hireling fleeth because he is an hireling, and careth not for the sheep. I am the good Shepherd, and know my sheep, and am known of mine. As the Father knoweth me, even so know I the Father: and I lay down my life for the sheep. And other sheep I have which are not of this fold: them also I must bring, and they shall hear my voice, and there shall be one fold and one shepherd."

1 PET. v. 4.

"And when the chief Shepherd shall appear, ye shall receive a crown of glory that fadeth not away."

"My Shepherd is the Lamb,
The living Lord who died!
With all that's truly good, I am
Most plenteously supplied!
He richly feeds my soul
With manna from above,
And leads me where the rivers roll,
Of everlasting love.

"He seeks me when I stray;
Directs my every path;
And when I walk through death's dark way,
Draws near with rod and staff.
My table He doth spread
In presence of my foes;
With oil He doth anoint my head;
My cup with wine o'erflows.

"Goodness and mercy wait
On all my steps through life;
They 'll bear me to the heavenly gate,
And set me free from strife.
Then I my Shepherd's care
Shall praise; my Host adore;
And in His Father's house shall share
True bliss for evermore!"

ANON.

THE GOOD SHEPHERD.

THE preceding emblems of Jesus are taken partly from objects of the external and inanimate creation, and partly from incidents in the history and institutes of the economy of the Jews. In addition to these, however, a very beautiful and instructive class of emblems is borrowed from the ordinary occupations of human life. Of this latter class, there is none more frequently employed in Scripture, or more expressive of condescension and grace on the part of Jesus towards His people, than that of a *shepherd*.

The scenes and occupations of pastoral life have been almost universally endeared to the hearts of men, by many sweet and picturesque associations. Accordingly, in every age, the poet has selected them as his darling theme, and lavished on their illustration and their eulogy, all his tenderness of sentiment and melody of verse. To the Jews, however, the similitude of a shepherd must have been peculiarly interesting, not only from the circumstance, that theirs was a country, where the flocks were numerous, and the pastoral life was held in great repute, but also from its association with all that was most venerable and sacred in their ancestral history,—the patriarch founders of their race, their illustrious lawgiver, and many of the greatest and most glorious of their judges and their kings having followed this ancient and honourable calling.

To us, indeed, who inhabit a commercial country, and dwell in cities, the force and beauty of this similitude may not be so clearly apparent, or so deeply felt. Guided, however, by the light of Scripture, it is not difficult to discover various particulars of resemblance, which illustrate the suitableness of its application to our Lord.

We begin, then, by observing, that *He has purchased His flock by the shedding of His own blood.* "I am the good Shepherd," He says Himself; "the good Shepherd giveth His life for the sheep." In common with the rest of mankind, His flock had wandered from the fold, and exposed themselves to the deadly assaults of their crafty and cruel foes. Night, too, had overtaken them, and obscured every way of return. The thunders of heaven rolled over their heads, and the torrent of Jehovah's wrath threatened to overwhelm them in its waves. But, in this situation of imminent danger, and utter helplessness, "when there was no eye to pity, and no arm to help," did the Good Shepherd fly on the wings of love to seek and to save them. "Though he was in the form of God, and thought it not robbery to be equal with God, he made himself of no reputation, and took upon him the form of a servant, and was made in the likeness of men; and being found in fashion as a man, he humbled himself, and became obedient unto death, even the death of the cross." "All we, like sheep, had gone astray; we had turned every one to his own way; but the Lord laid on him the iniquity of us all." Thus hath He opened up a new way of access and admission to the fold, and removed every obstacle that opposed their return. He has "saved His flock, and they shall no more be a prey."

Here, then, we have a proof of incalculable

force and magnitude, that Jesus is the Good Shepherd. For, "greater love hath no man than this, that a man lay down his life for his friends." But the conduct of Jesus in dying for His sheep, evinces a condescension and love, which cast into darkness all the noblest instances, in which human friends and earthly relatives have counted it "a sweet and sacred thing to die," in ransom for souls dearer to them than their own. For, not only was His life infinitely more valuable than all the lives of men or of angels, but there was not even the shadow of a claim on the part of those, for whom He so cheerfully laid it down. With the single exception of the misery in which they lay involved, and which was fitted to awaken in His bosom the sentiment of compassion, every thing in their original character and circumstances was fitted to *repel*, rather than to attract His regard. For, though bound by the strongest and most sacred ties to love and serve Him, they had, by rebelling against His righteous authority, rendered themselves the just and proper objects of His abhorrence and His vengeance. But such was His infinite mercy and grace, that He descended from the throne of heaven, not as the executioner of Divine vengeance, but as a messenger of peace, to publish, nay, to purchase and bestow salvation. "For God sent not his Son into the world, to condemn the world, but that the world through him might be saved."

But Jesus not only saves His flock from destruction, but becomes *their leader and guide.* As in oriental countries, the shepherd "goes before" his flock, to point out to them the way, so does the Good Shepherd lead His ransomed flock "in the paths of righteousness." The grand and merciful design of His mission into this waste howling wilderness, was "to seek and to save that which was lost." And, in prosecution of this design, He is still endeavouring, by His Word, His providence, and His Spirit, to turn us from the paths of ruin, and to restore us to the fold from which we have wandered. This exercise of His pastoral care is no less necessary than it is gracious; for, notwithstanding that those obstacles, which opposed the hope of return, have been completely removed, and we are freely invited to enter His fold, yet such is our natural aversion to spiritual things, that, if left to ourselves, we could never retrace our steps, but must continue, during the whole course of our earthly pilgrimage, to wander on, amongst those dark mountains on which our feet had stumbled, as sheep having no shepherd. "The carnal mind is enmity against God: for it is not subject to the law of God, neither indeed can be."

Even when we have been numbered among the ransomed flock of the Good Shepherd, and obtained admission into His fold, His guidance is as necessary as before. "The way of man is not in himself. It is not in man that walketh to direct his steps." During their pilgrimage towards the pastures of eternity, the flock of Jesus are not beyond the reach of temptation, or the assaults of spiritual danger. For there is not one of them, whom painful experience teaches not, that there lurks within him by nature, a constant proneness to err, and that ofttimes, through his own weakness, and negligence, and still remaining depravity, the pleasures of the world, the lusts of the flesh, and the pride of life, have enticed him beyond the pale of safety, and betrayed him into the snares and pitfalls by which his path is everywhere beset. Such, however, is the unwearied beneficence of our Celestial Shepherd, that, even when His flock have erred and strayed most widely from the straight and narrow path, instead of leaving them as a prey to the destroyer, He seeks them out in the wilderness, extricates them from every difficulty and danger, and graciously restores their souls, saying unto them, "I will heal your backslidings. I will love you freely." It is thus that He not only leads them at first from the world into His fold, but, from their returnings to the world, conducts them back into His fold again, and causes them to walk habitually in the paths of purity and peace.

Jesus also *feeds His flock with food convenient for them.* In His Word and ordinances, there is a copious and never-failing supply provided for their support and refreshment. These are, indeed, to them, as "pastures of tender grass," and "waters of quietness."

How rich and ample a pasturage is the field of *Scripture truth!* Whatever may be our condition and circumstances in the world, never can we fail to find in it a most suitable and seasonable portion. What food is to the body, that is this truth to the believer's spirit. It is the divine aliment of His renewed nature, being abundantly stored with all that is fitted to preserve and strengthen the spiritual life—with "doctrine, and reproof, and correction, and instruction in righteousness."

Nor are the oracles of His truth the only pastures, in which the Good Shepherd feeds His flock. As a provident shepherd leads about his flock from one verdant spot of pasturage to another, and gives them a pleasant diversity of food, so the Shepherd of souls has wisely appointed various means of grace for our sanctification and improvement. Accordingly, in the exercises of *social and secret prayer*, often do believers, in blessed experience, find that spiritual sustenance and consolation, after which their souls are hungering and thirsting, even as the hart panteth after the water-brooks. They are satisfied with the fatness of God's house, and feel that it is good for them to draw near unto Him. "A day in His courts" they esteem "better than a thousand spent in the tents of wickedness."

But a still richer and more satisfying nourishment is supplied to their souls, in the sacred ordinance of the *Lord's supper.* Here, while they behold all the blessings of the New Covenant—the pardon of sin, peace, and reconciliation with God, adoption into His family, the gift of the Holy Ghost, the consequent sanctification of their nature, persevering grace, victory over death, redemption from the power of the grave, and everlasting life—flowing to them through the death of Christ, and sealed and secured to them by His blood, their souls are comforted and refreshed, and they "are fed as with marrow and fatness." Here, they, by faith, receive the body of Christ, which is "meat indeed," and His blood, which is "drink indeed;" the largest wishes of their souls are amply gratified, and every virtue and grace of the divine life is enlivened and invigorated. Their faith is increased, their repentance deepened, their love inflamed, their hope animated and brightened, their heavenly mindedness promoted, and their benevolence extends its kindest regards to the whole family of man. The elements of spiritual nourishment diffuse themselves throughout all their frame, and their hearts are pervaded with sensations of a "peace" which "passeth understanding," and "a joy that is unspeakable and full of glory." Such, in a greater or less degree, is the experience of every worthy communicant.

The spiritual nourishment, which thus flows from the Word of God, and the ordinances of His grace, is permanent in its nature, and perpetual in its efficacy. It renders the spirit, to which it has been imparted, a stranger to decay; and so abundant is the supply provided, that it cannot be diminished, neither can it be exhausted for ever. This is that living Bread, which came down from heaven, of which if any man eat he shall not die, but live for ever.

But Christ further exercises the pastoral office, in respect of *His constantly watching over and defending His flock.* As a faithful shepherd carefully guards his flock from harm, and rescues them from peril while passing through the rugged vales, where death lurks among the precipitous cliffs, and deep and dark ravines, or in the dens of the beasts of prey, so does the Redeemer give protection and security to the sheep of His pasture, while passing through the dangerous vales of life, or the dark valley of the hadow of death—the dim defile which leads from time and opens on eternity.

Although they be under the guidance of the Good Shepherd, it must not be forgotten, that they are still passing through the wilderness, where they are doomed to encounter the opposition of those numerous, powerful, and malignant enemies, with whom they are surrounded. Against these, however, the Good Shepherd has been pleased to provide the most ample protection. His eye is ever upon His ransomed flock; His ear is ever open to their cry; His everlasting arms are ever around and underneath them. In every season of conflict and peril, He stands by their side, and says, "Fear not, for I am with thee: be not dismayed, for I am thy God: I will strengthen thee, yea, I will help thee, yea, I will uphold thee with the right hand of my righteousness." Nothing can befall them, which He does not know, and which He does not render subservient to the good of their souls.

How great, then, is the security enjoyed by those, who have been brought under the ever-waking care of the Shepherd of Israel! "As the mountains are round about Jerusalem, so the Lord is round about his people, from henceforth, even for ever." According to His own blessed declaration, "He will never leave them nor forsake them." He continues to be their guardian even until death, neither does He fail to stand by them at that solemn period, but enters with them into the deep and darksome vale, and uses every means to sustain, to defend, and to encourage them. They know and *feel*, that He is still by their side. By the eye of faith, they behold, as it were, the light of His countenance arise, like the day-star on the darkness; and even when engaged amidst the awful solemnities of death, it seems as though they heard the tones of His friendly voice whispering unto them, "Fear not, for I have redeemed thee: I have called thee by thy name. Thou art mine. When thou passest through the waters I will be with thee, and through the rivers, they shall not overflow thee; when thou walkest through the fire thou shalt not be burned, neither shall the flame kindle upon thee, for I am the Lord thy God, the Holy One of Israel, thy Saviour." Thus cheered by His presence, and sustained by His promises, many of the humblest and feeblest of His flock, who, "through, fear of death were" perhaps "all their life-time subject to bondage," have in their last moments been enabled to triumph over the King of Terrors, and to make the darksome vale resound with their fearless song, "Yea, though I walk through the valley of the shadow of death, I will fear no evil, for thou art with me: thy rod and thy staff they comfort me."

The metaphor under consideration suggests still further, that Jesus *will at last conduct His flock into the everlasting mansions of rest and safety which He hath prepared for them.* "I give," says He, "unto my sheep eternal life, and they shall never perish, neither shall any pluck them out of my hand." His redeeming them with His blood, His guiding, feeding, and defending them, are all subservient to His bringing them to His home of joy and glory in the heavens. There, He is now preparing a place for them, while, by His Holy Spirit, He is preparing them for entering into the promised rest. And He will come again, and receive them to Himself, that where He is there they may be also. In that blessed abode, He will perfect all that concerneth them, and from every evil to which they were subjected on earth, they shall be completely, and for ever exempted.

Then, shall faith have given place to sight, and hope to fruition, and they shall not only be, but feel themselves safe within their Shepherd's fold. They shall go no more out for ever; and, guided by their Celestial Shepherd, they shall pass continually onwards to those greener pastures and more fruitful fields of the heavenly Canaan, where "they shall not hunger nor thirst, neither shall the heat nor the sun smite them; for he that hath mercy on them shall lead them; even by the springs of water he shall guide them." "For the ransomed of the Lord shall return and come to Zion with songs and everlasting joy upon their heads; they shall obtain joy and gladness, and sorrow and sighing shall flee away." What tongue can describe, or mind conceive the ecstatic emotions of their souls, on entering those glorious and everlasting mansions of the Lord's redeemed? With what ineffable delight, will they congratulate themselves on their safe arrival there! What boundless and unmingled bliss will they experience! And with what ever increasing joy and gratitude, will they unite in the triumphant and eternal song of praise! "Unto him that loved us, and washed us from our sins in his own blood, and hath made us kings and priests unto God, and his Father, to him be glory and dominion for ever and ever."

Reader, while thus contemplating the Son of God, in the character of the Good Shepherd, have you the evidence within yourself, that you have been numbered among His chosen and blood-bought flock? Be it yours to improve aright your exalted privilege. While deeply grateful for His goodness, in taking you into His fold, and providing for you whatever is really necessary to your true enjoyment and felicity; rely with more implicit confidence upon His care; endeavour to feel more strongly the obligation of living by the faith of Him; and amidst all the toils and trials, the faintings and sorrowings of your desert-pilgrimage, take comfort from the thought, that He is ever with you, that He has the direction of all your paths, and that, ere long, He will bring you *in safety* to the promised land.

"Loving Shepherd, kind and true,
  Wilt Thou not in pity come
To Thy lamb? As shepherds do,
  Bear me in Thy bosom home;
Take me hence from earth's annoy
To Thy home of endless joy.

"See how I have gone astray
  In this earthly wilderness:
Come and take me soon away
  To Thy flock who dwell in bliss,
And Thy glory, Lord, behold,
Safe within Thy heavenly fold.

"For I fain would gaze on Thee,
  With the lambs to whom 't is given,
That they feed from danger free,
  In the happy fields of heaven;
Praising Thee, all terrors o'er,
Never can they wander more.

"Here I live in sore distress,
  Fearing, watching, hour by hour;
For my foes around me press,
  And I know their craft and power;
Lord, Thy lamb can never be
Safe one moment but with Thee.

"O Lord Jesus, let me not
  'Mid the ravening wolves e'er fall,
Help me as a shepherd ought,
  That I may escape them all;
Bear me homeward in Thy breast,
To Thy fold of endless rest."

ANGELUS, 1657.

The Physician.

Jerem. viii. 22.

"Is there no balm in Gilead? is there no Physician there? why then is not the health of the daughter of my people recovered?"

Luke v. 31, 32.

"And Jesus answering, said unto them, They that are whole need not a Physician; but they that are sick. I came not to call the righteous, but sinners to repentance."

Luke iv. 18.

"The Spirit of the Lord is upon me, because he hath anointed me to preach the gospel to the poor; he hath sent me to heal the broken-hearted, to preach deliverance to the captives, and recovering of sight to the blind, to set at liberty them that are bruised."

Heb. ix. 13, 14.

"For if the blood of bulls and of goats, and the ashes of an heifer sprinkling the unclean, sanctifieth to the purifying of the flesh; how much more shall the blood of Christ, who through the eternal Spirit offered himself without spot to God, purge your conscience from dead works to serve the living God?"

1 Pet. ii. 24.

"Who his own self bare our sins in his own body on the tree, that we, being dead to sins, should live unto righteousness: by whose stripes ye were healed."

John vi. 27.

"For him hath God the Father sealed."

"Deep are the wounds which sin has made,
Where shall the sinner find a cure?
In vain, alas! is nature's aid,
The work exceeds all nature's pow'r.

"Sin, like a raging fever, reigns,
With fatal strength on ev'ry part;
The dire contagion fills the veins,
And spreads its poison to the heart.

"And can no sov'reign balm be found?
And is no kind physician nigh,
To ease the pain, and heal the wound,
Ere life and hope for ever fly?

"There is a great Physician near;
Look up, O fainting soul, and live;
See, in His heav'nly smile appear,
Such aid as nature cannot give!

"See, in the Saviour's dying blood,
Life, health, and bliss, abundant flow
'Tis only this dear sacred flood
Can ease thy pain, and heal thy woe.

"Sin throws in vain its pointed dart;
For here a sov'reign cure is found;
A cordial for the fainting heart,
A balm for ev'ry painful wound."

STEELE

THE PHYSICIAN.

TO this designation, even in its literal signification, our blessed Saviour, while on earth, amply proved His title, "going about healing all manner of sickness, and all manner of diseases among the people." These works of benevolence, however, only afforded an evidence and an emblem of His spiritual character. The grand and merciful design of His mission unto this world was, that He might heal the souls of men from sin, which like a loathsome, distressing, and fatal disease, had deranged and vitiated their whole spiritual frame, and restore them to spiritual health, life, and happiness. Accordingly, He is frequently represented in Scripture, as the great *Physician of souls*—an appellation, the propriety of which will be clearly and fully perceived from the following considerations.

He has been divinely appointed to this im-

portant office. An earthly physician must be first examined and proved by competent authority, ere he can obtain a *diploma* entitling Him to practise the art of healing. Now, to the high office of recovering men from the disease of sin, Jesus Christ has been appointed by Him who is the sovereign Lawgiver, and the infallible Judge. "He took not this honour on himself, but was called of God, as was Aaron." Accordingly, at the commencement of His public ministry, part of the passage, which He read in the synagogue, and applied to Himself, contained His divine appointment to the office which He sustained. "The Spirit of the Lord is upon me; because he hath anointed me to preach the gospel to the poor; he hath sent me to heal the broken-hearted, to preach deliverance to the captives, and recovering of sight to the blind, to set at liberty them that are bruised." And when asked regarding His commission, or by what authority He cured the blind, the lame, the deaf, the dumb, and those possessed with devils, He asserted, that these miracles themselves proved, that He had come forth from God. "The works which the Father hath given me to finish, the same works that I do bear witness of me that the Father hath sent me. And the Father himself, which hath sent me, hath borne witness of me."

He has provided a remedy of transcendent efficacy. Long before His appearance on earth, it was predicted respecting the nature and effects of His atoning death—"In that day, there shall be a fountain opened to the house of David, and to the inhabitants of Jerusalem, for sin and for uncleanness." And when, in "the fulness of time," He poured forth His precious blood on the cross of Calvary, the ancient oracle was completely fulfilled; for the streams, which then flowed from His pierced side, are of boundless efficacy, in cleansing both from the guilt, and power of sin. This precious blood is the balm, which He hath provided to restore soundness to our sin-stricken nature.

In order to its being effectual, however, it is essential that it be applied to the soul, by the agency of the Holy Spirit. This was emblematically set forth under the Mosaic ritual, by the sprinkling of the blood of the sacrifices, and particularly, in the cleansing of the leper. Hence, the blood of Jesus is styled in Scripture, "the blood of sprinkling;" and we are exhorted to draw near unto God, "having our hearts sprinkled from an evil conscience." Such is the inherent virtue of this blood, that wherever it is thus applied to the sinner's soul by the Spirit, it is able to cleanse it from the foulest transgressions, and to restore it to moral health and vigour. "Purge me," said the Psalmist, "and I shall be clean; wash me, and I shall be whiter than snow." And, in every age of the world, its resistless efficacy has been realised, in the experience of thousands of our race who have trusted in it. It has been had recourse to, in the most extreme cases—by persons, who were farthest gone in the leprosy of sin, and had longest nourished its virulence—and they attested its efficacy. Nor shall its virtue ever be diminished. Even unto the end of the world, diseases of every degree of virulence, and at every stage, may be completely, and for ever removed by it; for Christ "is able to save to the uttermost all who come unto God by Him, seeing He ever liveth to make intercession for them."

It can hardly be necessary to remind the Christian reader, that the mode in which the

Spirit applies this efficacious remedy to the soul, is *by working faith in us.* It can profit us nothing, therefore, except we believe. As a medicine, in order to benefit a patient, must be taken by him, so the blood of Christ can have no salutary effect on those to whom it is proposed, unless there be a particular application of the merit of it to their souls. It is by faith in Christ alone, that we can obtain the healing, the life, the salvation which we require.

He is possessed of infinite skill. An earthly physician must not only be provided with proper remedies, but know also how to render them effectual. For this end, it is necessary that he should understand the anatomy of the human body, and the nature of the various diseases to which it is incident. He should be acquainted with the constitution of the patient, and the peculiar habits which he has contracted. Moreover, he should possess an accurate knowledge of the powers and virtues of medicines, and be skilful in dispensing and applying them. All these qualifications, the great Physician of souls possesses in an indefinite degree. "His understanding is infinite." He perfectly "knoweth our frame," and "needeth not that any man should testify to Him; for He knoweth what is in man." He knows all the maladies and distresses of our souls, with all their diversified forms and symptoms. He is intimately acquainted with our mental and moral constitution, and clearly discerns what are the most proper remedies to be employed for our recovery, and at what precise time, and in what quantity, they should be admini-stered. The skill of our heavenly Physician being unquestionable, it follows, that we may, with perfect confidence, commit the cure of our souls into His hands, saying unto Him, as did the leper who came to Him while He was yet on earth, "Lord, if Thou wilt Thou canst make me clean."

He is possessed of infinite power and compassion. He has resources adequate to every emergency, and is able to heal those in whom the spiritual malady has assumed its most malignant and inveterate form. He has but to say, "I will, be thou clean," and straightway the leprosy of the soul will be thoroughly and effectually taken away. "All power is given unto Him in heaven, and on earth," and, "with Him all things are possible."

And His compassion is equal to His power. "He will have mercy on His afflicted." "Like as a father pitieth his children, so the Lord pitieth them that fear Him."

> "Those that are broken in their heart,
> And grieved in their minds,
> He healeth; and their painful wounds
> He tenderly upbinds."

"In all our afflictions he is afflicted." From His experience of human trials and temptations, He has collected an unbounded store of sympathy for those whom "He is not ashamed to call His brethren." For "we have not an High-Priest which cannot be touched with the feeling of our infirmities; but was in all points tempted, like as we are, yet without sin." If, with one hand, He extends to us a bitter potion, with the other, He upholds, strengthens, and consoles us. "He lifts up the weak hands, and supports the feeble knees." "He will not break the bruised reed, nor quench the smoking flax, till He bring forth judgment unto victory."

He is very generous and disinterested. Many, in seeking a cure for their bodily diseases, ruin their worldly estate. Like the woman, who was healed by touching Christ's garment, they "spend all their living on physicians," and yet cannot "be healed of any." But, as she received His healing influence, without any payment or return, offered or expected, even so the cure of the soul's malady, by the merit and work of the Saviour, is emphatically a free gift. No mercenary motive, or interested aim, ever influences Him, on any occasion. He seeks not ours, but us. His sole object is to do us good. Besides, His skill is far too precious, His medicines far too valuable, to be purchased. "Come," He says, "and buy them, without money and without price." Nay, such is His condescension and kindness, that ofttimes does He come to the sick without being sent for, and entreats them to accept of that healing balm, without which, He knows, they must perish eternally. "He is found of them who sought not after Him."

He is accessible at all times, and in all places. An earthly physician, when we stand most deeply in need of his counsel and aid, may be at so great a distance, or have such a multiplicity of cases devolving on him, that before we can secure his services, it may be too late. Not so is it, however, with our celestial Physician. The throne of His grace is always accessible; and, of the countless myriads of souls that are looking unto Him from all parts of the wide world, there is not one beyond the reach of His aid. To all, He is a Physician "at hand, and not afar off"—"a very present help in trouble." "Lo!" saith He, "I am with you alway, even unto the end of the world." "I will never leave, I will never forsake you." "He, who hath known my name, shall call upon me, and I will answer him! I will be with him in trouble; I will deliver him and honour him." From the utmost corner of the land, our prayer will find its way even to His seat. Swifter than an angel, it enters heaven; and, whatever its request may be, like Jacob at Peniel, it has the power of a prince, and prevails.

How deeply grateful should we be to that heavenly Physician, who hath saved us from the most loathsome and deadly disease with which our nature can be affected! "Bless the Lord, O my soul! and all that is within me bless his holy name. Bless the Lord, O my soul, and forget not all his benefits; who forgiveth all thine iniquities; who healeth all thy diseases; who redeemeth thy life from destruction; who crowneth thee with lovingkindness and tender mercies; who satisfieth thy mouth with good things; so that thy youth is renewed like the eagle's."

We may hence also infer, with what perfect confidence we should follow the prescriptions of our spiritual Physician, who, as we have seen, is not only divinely appointed, but, in every respect, qualified to effect our cure. It is true, that our restoration to spiritual health may not be immediate, nor, indeed, is this to be expected; for the diseases of the soul are ever inveterate, and grow into habits, which can only be overcome by undergoing the discipline, which He has appointed, and which extends over the whole course of our mortal lives. Accordingly, the best of men, so long as they continue in the present world, are not free from occasional transgressions. But, in due time, our heavenly Physician will "perfect that which concerneth us," and introduce us into a world of which "the inhabitants shall not say, I am sick," for "the people that dwell therein shall be forgiven their iniquity."

But some of my readers may not yet have

made application to this Physician. Consider, then, that you must perish, and that eternally, if you continue to despise Him and His prescriptions. This assuredly will be the end of that disease, which is now preying on your very vitals. You may not, indeed, be conscious that you are labouring under its malignant influence, but this very circumstance is one of its most dangerous symptoms. Meanwhile, it retains its deadly hold of your hearts, and is increasing in virulence; and, if repentance and faith intervene not, it will hasten you on to the "death which never dies." There is only One in all the wide universe, who can save you, even Jesus Christ, whose blood is able to wash away your sin, and to heal your soul. Come, then, to Him, that you may not perish, but have everlasting life. Come, without hesitation, for His invitation is free; and without delay, for the time is short, and every moment that you spend without applying to Him only increases your danger. May the Lord Himself enable you to welcome the glad tidings, that there is "balm in Gilead, and that there is a Physician there."

"Oh, tender mercy's art divine!
Thy sorrow proves the cure of mine!
Thy drooping wounds, Thy woeful smart,
Allay the bleedings of my heart;
Thy death, in death's extreme of pain,
Restores my soul to life again."

PARNELL.

"Behold the leprous Jew,
Oppress'd with pain and grief,
Pouring his tears at Jesus' feet,
For pity and relief.

"'O speak the word,' he cries,
'And heal me of my pain;
Lord, Thou art able, if Thou wilt,
To make a leper clean.'

"Compassion moves His heart;
He speaks the gracious word;
The leper feels his strength return,
And all his sickness cured.

"To Thee, dear Lord, I look,
Sick of a worse disease;
Sin is my painful malady,
And none can give me ease.

"But Thy Almighty grace
Can heal my leprous soul:
O bathe me in Thy precious blood,
And that will make me whole."

STENNETT.

"When, by the busy crowd of life
Too often press'd and throng'd,
And in their rude and selfish strife
Both overlook'd and wrong'd;

"How sweet to know, Faith's lightest touch
The watchful Saviour feels,
And healing, in reply to such,
Into the suff'rer steals.

"Oft through the world we smoothly go
Hiding some secret care,
Our nearest, dearest, may not know
Which God alone can share.

"We mingle with the busy throng,
They pass unheeding by
They bear us in their tide along
We commune with the sky.

"Saviour, it is Thy people's bliss
To feel Thy care for them,
And, while the crowd Thy mercy miss,
To touch Thy garment's hem,

"Friends may mistake, or foes may slight,
Thyself not seem to see,
One touch of faith, however light,
Will find its way to Thee.

"And Thou wilt give, when sorrow pleads,
'Good comfort' to the soul,
The healing it so sorely needs,
The Faith which makes it whole."

MONSELL.

Conclusion.

CANT. v. 10, 16.

"My beloved is white and ruddy, the chiefest among ten thousand. His mouth is most sweet; yea, he is altogether lovely. This is my beloved, and this is my friend, O daughters of Jerusalem."

PS. xlv. 2.

"Thou art fairer than the children of men; grace is poured into thy lips; therefore God hath blessed thee for ever."

JOHN i. 14.

"And the Word was made flesh, and dwelt among us, (and we beheld his glory, the glory as of the only-begotten of the Father,) full of grace and truth."

I PET. i. 8.

"Whom having not seen, ye love; in whom, though now ye see him not, yet believing, ye rejoice with joy unspeakable, and full of glory."

JUDE 25.

"To the only wise God, our Saviour, be glory and majesty, dominion and power, both now and ever. Amen."

"Go, worship at Immanuel's feet;
See in His face what wonders meet;
Earth is too narrow to express
His worth, His glory, or His grace.

"Nor earth, nor seas, nor sun, nor stars,
Nor heaven, His full resemblance bears;
His beauties we can never trace,
Till we behold Him face to face.

"Oh, let me climb those higher skies,
Where storms and darkness never rise;
There He displays His power abroad,
And shines and reigns, th' incarnate God."

COWPER.

CONCLUSION.

IN addition to those we have illustrated, it were an easy, and it would be a pleasing occupation, to bring before the reader many other beautiful similitudes, by which the sacred writers set forth, in a not less interesting and attractive point of view, the glory and grace of Him, who is the Son of the Highest, and the Saviour of men. The field of Scripture truth, however, is adorned and beautified by such a rich profusion of this kind of imagery, that our limits could obviously admit only of a *selection*. Let us hope, that what has been advanced may induce every reader to gather diligently for himself. The study of Scripture metaphors of any kind is, doubtless, interesting and attractive. Addressing the mind, through the medium of the senses, such word-pictures are adapted to arrest the attention; the imagination is engaged in discovering their beauty, and admiring their aptitude; while they rivet themselves in the memory, by the impressive manner in which they convey their meaning to the heart. But, inasmuch as every part of Scripture is made subservient to the striking exhibition of "Jesus Christ, and Him crucified," the metaphorical diction employed to set forth the beauties of the principal figure in the picture, ought unquestionably to hold a corresponding prominence in all our biblical studies. And the more constantly we contemplate Him in His true character, as exhibited either in the plain or the figurative expressions employed by the sacred writers, the more closely shall we, by the divine blessing, be assimilated to His image, and the more meet shall we, in the end, be found for "seeing Him *as he is.*"

"How sweet the Name of Jesus sounds
In a believer's ear!
It soothes his sorrows, heals his wounds,
And drives away his fear.

"It makes the wounded spirit whole,
And calms the troubled breast:
'Tis manna to the hungry soul,
And to the weary rest.

"Dear Name! the rock on which I build,
My shield and hiding-place;
My never-failing treas'ry fill'd
With boundless stores of grace.

"By Thee my prayers acceptance gain,
Although with sin defiled;
Satan accuses me in vain,
And I am own'd a child.

"Jesus! my Shepherd, Kinsman, Friend,
My Prophet, Priest, and King;
My Lord, my Life, my Way, my End,
Accept the praise I bring.

"Weak is the effort of my heart,
And cold my warmest thought;
But when I see Thee as Thou *art*,
I'll praise Thee as I ought.

"Till then I would Thy love proclaim
With ev'ry fleeting breath,
And may the music of Thy name
Refresh my soul in death."

NEWTON.

"Join all the glorious names
Of wisdom, love, and power,
That ever mortals knew,
That angels ever bore;
All are too mean to speak *His* worth,—
To set my Saviour's glories forth.

"Great Prophet of my God!
My tongue would bless Thy name;
By Thee the joyful news
Of our salvation came;
The joyful news of sin forgiven,
Of hell subdued, and peace with heaven.

"Jesus, my great High Priest!
Offer'd His blood and died;
My guilty conscience seeks
No sacrifice beside:
His precious blood did once atone,
And now it pleads before the throne.

"All hail, almighty Lord!
My Conqueror and King!
Thy sceptre and Thy sword—
Thy reigning grace I sing;
Thine is the power! Behold I sit
In willing bonds beneath Thy feet.

"Should all the hosts of death,
And powers of hell unknown,
Put their most dreadful forms
Of rage and mischief on,—
A feeble saint shall win the day,
Though death and hell obstruct the way."

WATTS.

"To Christ, the Lord, let every tongue
Its noblest tribute bring;
When He's the subject of the song,
Who can refuse to sing!

"Majestic sweetness sits enthroned
Upon His awful brow;
His head with radiant glories crown'd,
His lips with grace o'erflow.

"No mortal can with Him compare
Among the sons of men;
Fairer He is than all the fair
That fill the heavenly train.

"He saw me plunged in deep distress,
And came to my relief;
For me He bore the shameful cross,
And carried all my grief.

"His hand a thousand blessings pours
Upon my guilty head;
His presence cheers my darkest hours,
And guards my sleeping bed.

"To Him I owe my life and breath,
And all the joys I have:
He makes me triumph over death,
And saves me from the grave.

"To heaven, the place of His abode,
He brings my weary feet;
Shews me the glories of my God,
And makes my joy complete.

"Since from His bounty I receive
Such proofs of love divine,
Had I a thousand hearts to give,
Lord, they should all be Thine!"

STENNET.

"Praise God, from whom all blessings flow;
Praise Him, all creatures here below;
Praise Him above, angelic host;
Praise Father, Son, and Holy Ghost."

THE END.

CPSIA information can be obtained
at www.ICGtesting.com
Printed in the USA
LVHW100447110522
718424LV00003B/273

9 783375 006594